"Not one of us is safe. And there are things…they look small enough sometimes too…by which some of us are totally and completely undone."

—Joseph Conrad
Lord Jim

MAN IN A BLACK CAR

by
Brad Viking

PublishAmerica
Baltimore

© 2006 by Brad Viking.
All rights reserved. No part of this book may be reproduced, stored in a retrieval system or transmitted in any form or by any means without the prior written permission of the publishers, except by a reviewer who may quote brief passages in a review to be printed in a newspaper, magazine or journal.

First printing

All characters appearing in this work are fictitious. Any resemblance to real persons, living or dead, is purely coincidental.

At the specific preference of the author, PublishAmerica allowed this work to remain exactly as the author intended, verbatim, without editorial input.

ISBN: 1-4241-4610-0
PUBLISHED BY PUBLISHAMERICA, LLLP
www.publishamerica.com
Baltimore

Printed in the United States of America

Man in a Black Car

1

Harlan pulled up at the Starlite Café just as dawn was breaking. He slumped into a corner booth, ordered his usual, and poked at a puddle of catsup with his fries.

This was the hour the guard changed. When the night creatures who had gathered began to slip back into the darkness...before the first rays of sunlight could reach out and touch their pasty skin. Harlan watched them...one by one...pay their bills...and scatter like cockroaches into the night. Seeking the darkness...the oblivion...the anonymity.

His mind was on Holly and the reasons she died. When do you admit defeat, he wondered. When have you taken enough blows to the head that you know it's time to hug the mat...take the count...and get the hell out of town. It's a tough call...that returning home tail-between-the-legs humility. It means admitting you ain't got what it takes. But it also means survival. So what is it that would make someone prefer to turn blue with a needle in her arm...buy a one-way ticket to oblivion...instead of a ticket on the midnight train to Georgia?

Harlan had no answer to that one.

He had worked the Hollywood beat a long time. Watched the seekers come and the seekers go. Watched so many of them self-destruct in quest of fame. The only way to kill the dream, it seemed, was to kill the dreamer…like a moth making a kamikaze dive into the flame. In death, at least, was peace from that damnable star-making machinery.

* * *

The Starlite was a different crowd. Harlan understood them. Most had been beaten up enough to know they didn't have what it takes in this town. And they were O.K. with that. O.K. with anonymity. They had learned to avert their eyes when they passed that sign on the hill. Odysseus shutting out the seductive lure of the Sirens. They were no longer driven by dreams of fame…no longer jonesing for their fifteen ticks. There was a kind of wisdom there.

It was a wisdom that Harlan had learned early-on himself…the day he came home from school with a shiner.

"Bully-boys gave you a pump and a lug, huh?"

"Yeah…sorry Pop."

"Nothing to be sorry about. You remember what I told you?"

"Yeah, you've got to know when to quit. Otherwise they remember you as the guy on the mat."

"Yeah." One shoulder of his father lurched in a strange spasm as he dispensed his wisdom.

Harlan squinted through his puffy eye.

"But Pop…"

His dad nodded, elbows in, soaking up the next punch.

"I understand. You want to know if it's hard to quit?"

His father gave him a long weary look over the length of a pipe crusted with soot, his craggy face eroded by time. It was the look of a man who had fought a lot of battles, but had learned to survive through ways other than brute force. It was hard won turf.

"Well, not if you're the guy on the mat."

* * *

It was sage advice for a kid smaller than the others, a shrimp getting cuffed by the schoolyard bullies. But as the years passed...and Harlan waited for that growth spurt...he grew tired of being easy pickings. A lot of displaced anger began building up inside him. He felt powerless against the forces that oppressed him for no apparent reason.

Then came the day he got beat up so bad his eye was permanently damaged. A dilated pupil that left him with a spooky looking glint...like broken glass. That was the day he saw a new side to his father. Soberly, without a word, Pop took down an old pair of boxing gloves. He fitted them on the young boy.

"What I'm going to teach you, Harlan, is something I learned from my Dempsey days. He was a champ. He turned lightweights into hamburger with his fists. And some of them never wanted to box again. I know. I was one of them."

Harlan didn't end up on the mat much after that. And the bully-boys in the school yard learned to keep their distance from the scrappy kid with the mean right hook. The kid was small, but he had a ferocity about him now that sent a chill into the darkest center of their predatory hearts. They could still take him down, but they were going to lose some vital organ in the process.

* * *

Harlan felt a warm glow of nostalgia burn inside him as he gazed at the last cold French fry marooned in a puddle of ketchup. From what he could see, the night crowd at the Starlite were guys left on the mat. Poor saps who never had Pop to teach them how to fake with the left…and deliver a take-down punch with the right.

Or maybe they just never felt the rage he felt when backed up against a wall. Never got desperate enough to tap into that blighted well inside them…the muddy banks where low-slung leathery creatures slip into the water…white teeth slashing at the crimson entrails of their oppressors.

2

The Man in the Black Car slammed his brakes...veered to a stop beside the road. He ran back to where he'd heard the *thump*. But no one was there. He searched frantically up and down the highway. Beside the road. Nothing. No indication of anyone ever being hit. He was dazed...disbelieving as he stood there in the headlights...soaked to the skin from the thick downpour...the wiper blades beating in a strange kind of counterpoint to the storm.

All he could do was return to the car still idling beside the road...steam rising from the hot engine as the rain splattered across the hood...and drive back down Pacific Coast Highway to L.A.

* * *

The shock of that night on PCH...the echo of that *thump*...it managed to find a hole in the smooth surface of his conscience. Slip through and worm its way into his heart.

That was the night Harlan began to ride the saws. The first night he had the black car dream. It had shattered him…changed him deeply. In his sleep the image played over and over.

What had triggered it? Harlan had never had that kind of dream before. He kept his life well-ordered. Like a game of billiards. Only the crisp click of pool balls on a velvet green table. The solid smack of ivory on ivory…the clarity of the sound…pure and concise…his mind following the exact trajectory of each ball with mathematical precision.

But that was before the first muffled *thump*. Before his shoulder began that strange lurching motion…as if he was chafing inside an ill-fitting coat. And he hadn't been the same since.

* * *

Harlan picked up the grease-stained bill off the table…paid at the register…and called it a night.

When he got home he removed the .38 caliber revolver from his shoulder holster and set it on the table. His powerful fingers ran over the cold metal. It helped calm him. Then he hit the bed with the dead weight of a punchy contender…K.O.'ed and down for the count.

3

"What have you got?"

Lt. Eddie Azimuth pointed down from the balcony.

"Could be an accident. Could be homicide."

Harlan looked down at the broken, twisted body splayed across the jagged rocks below. He gave Azimuth a roll of the eyes.

"How many guys get naked and fall off their balcony by *accident?*"

He felt the burning sensation in his shoulder kick in. This time a cue that he'd been working too many hours on too little sleep.

He took a deep breath…listened to the crisp click of ivory on velvet somewhere in the back of his mind. He liked the logic of it. It's what made him a good detective. To Harlan it was a lot like solving crimes.

"Who is it?"

"Byron Slade. Power player. Big shot Hollywood agent."

"Sounds familiar."

"Had a certain stink about it."

"How's that?"

"He was the agent for that wannabe case you're working on. The one who O.D.ed the other night."

"Holly."

He remembered the blue arm...the silver bracelet dangling from her wrist.

* * *

Harlan skipped across the rough granite boulders as he followed Lt. Azimuth down to the beach. The seawall was put in after the last big storm to protect a posh row of Malibu homes from heavy surf. It cost the city a chunk, but these were the high-rollers of *The Industry* out here. They had clout.

Harlan was middle-aged...putting on a little weight...but he still had the deft moves of someone who knew his way around ocean waves. Some salt spray shot up...caught him mid-leap. It covered his face and he licked it from his lips. It tasted good. Reminded him of another place and time...*chubascos* kicking up a south swell off Mexico...and one wave in particular he'd tangled with that summer.

Azimuth pointed to the edge of the surf line. The naked body of the man lay half-buried in the sand. They both looked up at the balcony he'd tumbled from.

"What do you think?"

"Slade, you said?"

"Yeah."

"I just talked to him two days ago."

"Rumor has it you had to take a number if you wanted to kill this guy."

"Add me to the list."

As soon as he'd said it he felt the sharp burn in his shoulder again.

* * *

Something glittered in the Malibu moonlight.

"What is that?" asked Harlan.

"Looks like an Oscar, doesn't it?"

A wave washed over the body, swept away some of the sand. It was clear where the Oscar was imbedded.

"Weird, huh?"

Harlan grunted. His voice was edged with the weary buzz of burnt-out neon above a cheap motel.

"Not for Hollywood."

He nodded toward the side of town where he worked his normal beat.

"If the world ever needs an enema…that's where they'll stick the tube."

Seemed like he'd spent a lifetime over there. And all he ever ran across were low-lifes like Slade. He was ready for a change.

"By the book, Eddie. No wiggle room for their legal sleaze."

"It's a rich man's game, Harlan. You know that. They write checks and walk."

"Yeah. But just once. Just once I'd like to keep them from shoving Blind Justice off the curb and into the grillwork of their big fat limos."

4

From the street it was just another Hollywood agent's office overlooking the jugular of the Sunset Strip. But standing here...on Slade's stretch of the savanna...Harlan felt dangerously exposed. He was standing on ground zero of the predatory cosmos...and he could sense the bloodstains that had been scrubbed from the carpet.

One thing Harlan had learned in his fifty-three years...you're always on someone's menu. A mugger in the park. A snake in the jungle. Maggots in the grave. At every stage of life on the savanna there was someone out there licking their chops. Now...as he stood facing Byron Slade...he felt like he had just been added to the menu.

Slade's eyes had a sort of mad distraction to them...as if he were listening to the snap and crackle of ravenous beetles eating away the flesh from dead animals. Or perhaps it was young innocent larvae...the delectable morsels that lined the corridors outside.

MAN IN A BLACK CAR

* * *

According to a background on Slade, he had arrived on the Hollywood scene rather abruptly with "European credentials." But something about him told Harlan to keep the elbows in…protect his gut.

A swarthy gangster of a man…Slade sat sprawled in a huge leather chair at his desk. He waved Harlan in. Large, protruding eyes…dark as marble…examined him from under drooping lids while he berated some poor subordinate on the phone. His thick hands gestured wildly.

Harlan's crime-scene mind took a snapshot of the office. The man's hoof marks were all over it. Photos of himself with stars and sports celebrities festooned the walls…movers and shakers of every stripe. Stacks of scripts and 8 by 10 head shots of starlets cluttered his desk. A gleaming Oscar adorned one corner. Harlan sniffed the air, winced. A strange odor tainted the room.

* * *

The Agent slammed the phone down, turned to Harlan.
"Right here. That's the key to power in *this* town."
He pointed to the phone.
"You can't imagine the kind of hunger a phone arouses in jerk-off actors."
He paused, gave Harlan a quick once over.
"You're not an actor, are you?"
Harlan shook his head.
"Like Pavlov's dogs. He could make 'em salivate with a bell. I can do it with one phone call."
You could tell it got his pulse racing. He wiped some saliva off the edge of his lips.

Harlan offered a faint smile, flashed his shield.

"I know you're squeezed for time. Just need to ask a few questions about an actress you represented. Holly Corralini."

"Holly who?"

"Corralini."

"You said represent*ed*. Past tense. Is there something I should know."

"She O.D.'d a few nights back. Some dirty smack."

Harlan paused for it all to register.

Blank.

"You were at *her funeral...*" Harlan prompted.

"I go to a lot of funerals. High attrition rate in this town."

"It was raining at this one."

"Oh, yeah." His voice droned with vague indifference. "The studio sent its regrets."

Harlan felt a burning sensation in his shoulder. He reached, massaged the center of discomfort.

He showed Slade a photo of Holly.

"She was studying to be an actress."

Slade sniffed with contempt.

"*Actress.* Yeah, I remember. Another loser laboring under the delusion she had some kind of talent."

Slade scooped up a stack of head shots in his meaty hand.

"Do you know how many of these I get every week?"

Harlan sat grim and motionless as he watched Slade.

"Thousands. It's unbelievable. I don't know where they all come from. And every one of them thinks they're an 'actress.'"

He tossed the head shots back on the desk.

"Wannabes. That's all they are. They have no talent...no looks...no '*heat.*' Maybe a good set of tits. That's it. Sure, a few pop up to the surface like bloated fish. But for every one of those, there's a hundred more at the bottom...bones picked clean...sucked into the ooze of obscurity. Most of them end up fluffing dicks for the porn industry in the Valley."

A hefty diamond ring glinted in the sunlight as he clutched the Oscar that sat on his desk. He held it up.

"Now this...that's what the hot women in this town crave...a guy with thirteen inches of hard, stiff power."

"I wasn't aware they gave those to agents."

He punched up an old laugh track.

"Naw...found it in a pawn shop. Some washed-up actor hocked it to buy booze. I just keep it here. Adds credibility. Feel it. It's solid. That thing could crack a skull."

He leaned in earnestly toward Harlan, conspiracy in his voice.

"Besides, it helps get me laid."

It was that smirk. And the arrogant way he laughed. Harlan had heard it before. In the schoolyard when he was getting beat up. Already he hated this guy.

Slade leaned back, set down the statue.

"Take this Holly, for instance. Probably one that polished my Oscar so I got her a walk-on."

The smirk was dark...malevolent.

"Had more than a few under this desk. But that's what makes this business so sweet...the absolute power to make or break lives."

An old movie flickered to life in Harlan's mind...cracked and crumbling celluloid...the shape of a dark figure lurching through fog. A stark black and white image that stabbed into his memory. It was something that set his boyhood pulse racing as he crouched in the dark theater. Something he sensed would always be out there...something menacing and without remorse...bent on the destruction of softness and vulnerability. As a boy he never saw the features of that menace that emerged through the fog. But now, as a cop who knew the savagery at work on the streets, that dark figure suddenly took on a face. It was Slade's.

* * *

"How long has Holly been your client?"

Slade got up and strode over to a couch by the window. He ran his thick fingers over the leather as if it still radiated the heat from the latest victim.

"Dunno. Six, maybe eight months."

He punctuated his words with a smack of his fist on the leather.

"It's a hard-ball town, detective…you know that. Most of 'em just don't have staying power. They come apart like a three-dollar ukulele in the rain."

The agent straightened a photo on the wall. Bonding with some rock star.

"Like I said, she was a mediocre talent. Never could land much work for her. Haven't seen her in over a week at least."

He stretched out behind his desk again.

"A lot of them go into depression after awhile," he added.

"Can't handle the rejection. The ones like Holly…sometimes they take the easy way out."

Harlan felt that ache in his shoulder kick in. He pocketed his notes, straightened his coat, and headed for the door.

"That's all I need for now."

"But you know what?" Slade's voice followed him.

Harlan turned. There was that smirk again.

"There's always another one waiting to take her place."

That was the last time Harlan felt the burn in his shoulder. He managed to resist the compelling need to plant his knuckles in the man's bulbous face.

Just as well. Someone would beat him to it. Two nights later the man's body would drift up on a Malibu beach...a shiny gold Oscar stuffed up his arrogant ass.

5

Slow and rich as syrup pouring over southern-fried fritters. Harlan watched the shapely pair of legs descend from a sleek limo that had just pulled up at the Hollywood cemetery. She swiveled her way toward the gravesite where black umbrellas popped open to shield the rich and powerful from an unscripted L.A. drizzle. They gathered around the grave in muffled silence as a siren wailed and faded in the distance.

Harlan put down a copy of *The Hollywood Reporter* as he watched the exhaust of the limo puff like an expensive cigar. *People love to read about trouble in Paradise* he was thinking as he looked up through gray drizzle at the hill in the distance. It was that sign. That shabby piece of clapboard propped up like a cheap facade on the banks of the Volga. The Catherine the Great Tour. It sat there…heartless as ever…hissing its contempt for both the living and the dead…with little distinction between the two.

According to the *Reporter*, Holly's death was just another sad story of a naïf who failed to reconcile her dreams with reality. She made a desperate gamble to get her name on the marquee...made some "friends in high places." Harlan looked up, a cynical twist to his lips. In Industry-speak that meant polishing the knobs of the studio elite. But despite her intrigue...and all the sweet lamentations the press heaped on Holly's sad story...she had failed to make the cut.

Harlan knew all the plotting in this town wasn't written into scripts. As a cop he had learned to read between the lines. Back in the pack there was always another game going on. A game within a game played on a very sophisticated level by fast and subtle players. A cunning and cutthroat game...where lives are driven by obsession...and the stakes are lethal.

Maybe Holly had a little help on her way into the obituaries.

* * *

Harlan folded the *Reporter* and held it over his head as he circled the perimeter of mourners. He found a place at the edge of the crowd and began taking some mental notes.

Circling the black umbrellas...scanning faces through the drizzle...he suddenly stopped. There...just beneath one of the umbrellas...two gorgeous blue eyes were gazing at him. Not just gorgeous...ablaze and blue as an acetylene torch. For a split-second it threw him. Why was she watching him? Who was she? Did she belong to that gorgeous pair of legs that stepped out of the limo?

Then they were gone...slipped back beneath the anonymous huddle of black umbrellas. But there seemed to be something beyond that brief visual engagement.

As the crowd dispersed Harlan tried to catch sight of the woman. But she merged back into blackness...left the funeral unseen...and he was left with only a glimpse. Just one brief fragment of memory to remember her by.

6

Hurtling at ninety miles an hour down a slick road in the darkness, the vintage black Packard was a freight train. And the impact would be ugly if anything crossed its path.

But the driver was in no mood to care. He kept his foot on the gas, never slowed, pushing the odds, hoping luck would be on his side. In the silence his hands gripped the wheel, his mind floating free as he inhaled the nicotine-high from his cigarette. He felt...for a brief buoyant moment...absent of all dread...disengaged from the conflicts that had launched this troubled flight down the slick coastal road. In his mind, he felt in control of his destiny.

"Love is pure gold...and time a thief." The honeydew voice on the radio clung to the phrase...put some hurt behind it...doing all she could to sweep the night clean of the blues. A muted sax curved and distorted the anguish of the lyrics even more. The driver watched raindrops splatter against the glass in tune with the smoky voice before being swept away by the backbeat of

windshield wipers. Each arc gave him a brief glimpse into the void...brief moments of clarity before being washed away.

He glanced at the seat beside him, read the words on the perfumed card once again...words that had no place in the heart of a thug like him. He stubbed his cigarette into the ashtray, grabbed the card and crumpled it in his powerful hand.

Twenty years he had held out. For twenty years he had resisted the beautiful scent of that liquid that jostled quietly in the bottle beside him. But now it was coming after him...moonlight dancing on gold. He reached for the bottle...unscrewed the cap. The aroma filled the car as it slid down his throat...the beautiful warm glow flooding his body...his mind...drawing a merciful curtain between him and reality.

But in that split second...ahead...an unsuspecting shadow began to cross the asphalt slick with rain. Clutching a black umbrella...huddled beneath the protective shell...the figure stepped onto the road...

* * *

That's when Harlan McCoy heard the muffled *thump* that had been haunting his sleep every night. That strange *thump* that had become a loose grenade tumbling across the ground. It left him with that peculiar tic coiling through his shoulder, causing an odd snap of the neck...like adjusting an ill-fitting coat.

Harlan had developed enough surge capacity to handle the stress points of the job. But there were times when it broke down...when he had single-point failures. Hearing that *thump* was one of them. It snaked past all his Checkpoint Charlies...got in deep behind his lines...became an emotional rogue inside him.

It had been a week since he heard that solid *thump* in his dreams...saw the black distorted shape roll violently over the hood…the thick streaks of crimson smear the windshield in the rain. Was it only a dream? Where did it come from? Did it ever really happen?

7

Azimuth had run some background on Holly. Dixie's place on Franklin was one of her hangouts. Just the kind of dive where film students and wannabes could get their cheap fix of classic Hollywood.

Her real name was Patty Jo Flynn...but she called herself Dixie Stardust. Born dirt poor somewhere in the Bible Belt, she came to Hollywood in the Silent Era, made one or two major releases, and quickly faded back into oblivion. But she was the queen of a glorious and misbegotten past to a small clique of student film makers. They gathered here at least once a week to pay homage to their own personal Norma Desmond.

Arriving here when the sign still read HOLLYWOODLAND, Dixie's fortunes were not much better than another starstruck reject...Peg Entwhistle. Abandoned by fame, Peg took a nose dive to her death off the "H" of the sign on the hill. It was a long time ago. But the lure remained the same...the illusion of being loved by millions...egos basking at the sight of themselves on a forty-foot screen.

Dixie was a one-shot wonder back then, a vamp in some silent melodrama. But talkies came in and she was sabotaged...like many others...by the cat-scratch sound of her voice.

The kids who gathered here called her Norma Desmond. It wasn't meant to be kind, but Dixie was usually too drunk to feel the pin-pricks of their cruelty.

They figured her as half-mad. But for film students and Hollywood wannabes it was part of the lore. She *was* their Norma Desmond, clinging to the past, eyes glazed over with faded glory as she sat in her tattered robe, holding court for the remnants of her unwashed fellow seekers.

"*Vissi d'arte*," she was fond of saying in melodramatic tones, "I live for art." And her frail hands would rise to frame her face...pale white palms and slender fingers quivering at the edge of her cheeks. And her eyes rolled skyward...soft...fawn-like...as her voice paused reverently to utter the words. And in that moment a force-field of some kind fell over the room as they watched this soiled, fallen angel slip over the edge of reality and into a fantasy so deep and so real that it shamed all those who had dared to smirk at her condition.

They were witnessing a visitation from the other side of madness and even though it lasted for only a fleeting moment, it left a powerful and indelible impression on those who witnessed it. It was a dark warning for all those who pretended to the throne...for those who let their egos succumb to the lure of fame.

This is what awaits the also-rans her rum-drenched eyes were saying. You can hunch down by the phone and wait for *The Call*. But what if it never rings? That is the haunting question that Dixie posed for those neophytes who gathered here to mock her...but who left with a new kind of terror in their hearts...a terror instilled by the depths of her madness.

Even those who fancied themselves too hip, the ones who

slouched on the faded furniture and scoffed at her naiveté, were caught by surprise when she performed this ritual. And they would stop mid-sentence...caught in the sobering pathos, the poignancy of someone who had succumbed so completely to the Hollywood disease...

8

When Harlan arrived she was wearing a ragged pink peignoir with a feathery boa...and shuffled about her unkempt apartment in Jean Harlow mules, puffs of pink feathers that floated on the wisps of air stirred by the movement of her gnarled feet.

To counter the treason's of time she had festooned the apartment with fading mementos of her past glory...a framed poster of her films, some autographed head shots of screen idols from the silent era...a champagne glass from Ciro's. From time to time she would pause and mumble to herself as she moved among the faded memorabilia.

She got a chance for a "come-back" in *The Ladies of the Chorus*, a black-and-white B pic shot in 1948. Her voice was dubbed so she could carry it off. She fed a tape into a VCR and hopped up on her bed. A smile sneaked across her face.

> *We're the ladies of the chorus,*
> *here to sing and dance for you...*

She sang along as the movie opened with a chorus line shot. "There I am! That's me! Wasn't I a dish?" she blurted, pointing to a young woman with thin limbs and generously cut curves.

She could watch this tape a hundred times. Probably had. And as others in that chorus line rose to stardom, she couldn't imagine that she would remain an extra…for 52 years and counting.

* * *

Harlan spent a couple hours talking to Dixie. She continued showing off her memorabilia. Once, catching sight of herself in a mirror, she desperately started dabbing on more mascara…more lipstick…more layers of rouge…to hide the grotesque landscape her face had become.

"I really shouldn't look in mirrors anymore," she uttered with a shy casting of the eyes. "But then…" her voice rose with dramatic flair…"mirrors were *made* for glamorous stars like me."

Between the teacups full of cheap booze, she told him Holly had been there all right. She was cozy with one of the film students.

"He had one of those Russian names…Vladimir…or Ivan…something like that."

Then her eyes fluttered with a sort of mad distraction as she gazed off into the stage lights of her past.

"Did I ever tell you about the time I met a famous Russian director?"

* * *

Harlan remembered seeing her in a film once on late night television. A lot like Harlow, he recalled. In her prime, she was the kind of woman who could hit the emergency button in an elevator with her stiletto heel. In fact, if Harlow hadn't come on the scene when she did, Dixie might be the "It" girl everyone remembered. Instead, she was the "Who?" girl everyone had forgotten.

Harlan listened to her reminisce about the golden era of Hollywood, her voice rasping from cigarettes and booze. Onscreen her slim fingers had curled around the crystal stem of a champagne glass…wet and breathless as she brought the rim up to crimson lips…let the golden bubbles slide across the surface of her tongue. Smuggled secrets burst from her eyes in those close-ups. Now, it was all awash in a haze of delusion.

Everything he could glean from her that day amounted to little more than the fanciful mist of gin and vermouth. But Harlan decided to follow up on one lead…the Russian film student.

9

"Something to warm you up?" was all she said.

Carolina molasses. He'd always been a sucker for the lemon drop lure of a Southern drawl. Her voice strung the words out like a silk scarf drifting over naked skin. That...and the aroma of fresh-brewed coffee...slowly turned Harlan's head.

It was her. The blue eyes under the umbrella. Damn! Destiny was throwing strike balls. She was a key witness in the Holly O.D. case.

He tilted his gaze to the young actress. It was only a split second glance into the blue conflagration of those eyes...but it was long enough for him to know she had slipped in under his radar...into that combat zone where reason does battle with desire. A spilt honey sensation gushed up through his thighs...and uncoiled inside his heart...and began melting all the paved-over emotions he'd kept buried such a long, long time.

"Thanks," he replied. "Just what I needed."

She handed him the cup. Then...as if some puppet-master

pulled a string…she added a little spontaneous twitch of her body. A kind of soft powder-puff dab against the air. It was totally spontaneous…and totally charming.

That was it. He tried to invoke the code of the pool balls…the serene mathematical trajectory of each sphere as it rolled across velvet green. His way to stay cool. He knew that terrain. He trusted it. Six pockets. It had precision to it…the same precision as solving a crime.

But it wasn't working. She was bending his gravitational field with those acetylene blue eyes. And that little move she just did.

Harlan flashed his shield, introduced himself.

"Sorry to trouble you, but I need to talk to you about Holly. I understand she was a friend."

"That's O.K. I'd like to help."

"You work together long?"

"Just on this set. We're both trying to get a foot in the door."

He talked to her for twenty minutes. As she spoke he felt all the structural integrity of his years alone begin to weaken. It had been a long time since he'd met anyone that could do that to him.

* * *

"Something to warm you up?" was all she said.

It was all she needed to say…

Her name was Lana. He knew because she left it…and a phone number…on the napkin under the coffee.

10

Harlan sat at the kitchen table and stared at the phone number on the napkin. She was too gorgeous, he told himself. She was too young. She was another scary actress...conflicted, neurotic, intense. He went through the litany of every reason he shouldn't call her.

He replayed the entire day on the set.

"Damn."

His hand spun the chamber of his .38 revolver. Then he pulled out a cartridge and gripped its cold metal jacket in his fist. Striding toward the cue rack, he pulled down a custom stick and walked over to the pool table.

In matters of divining cosmic destiny...and the inherently messy decisions that had to do with women...Harlan had developed a Solomon-like protocol. A cool-headed course of action. Obviously, things of this magnitude couldn't be left to the simian mood-swings of a man's little head. He would trust his decision to the physics of a rolling billiard ball...the click of ivory on ivory. He would leave his decision to the pure laws of science.

He set up a shot glass at one end and a spoon wedged between two ivory balls at the other. Then he balanced the .38 slug on the scoop of the spoon. A man's destiny was about to ride on the single stroke of a custom cue.

"Make Willie Mosconi proud, baby."

The smooth maple slid across his skin…soaked up the shock…dispatched the cue ball with a sharp *crack*. The ball rolled smartly across velvet green…smacked the black eight. Copper on the slug's casing shimmered in the light as it somersaulted gracefully into the air. It moved with the athletic ease of a trapeze artist suspended mid-air. Then…a solid *ping* as the slug landed upright in the shot glass.

Harlan gazed at it for a long beat. The slug had spoken. His destiny was sealed. He reached and pulled the live round from the glass and slid it back into the chamber of his revolver.

Truth was, no matter how the slug would have divined his fate, Harlan knew once he dove into the pool of those cobalt blue eyes, he was doomed to make that call.

So much for the laws of science.

11

It was a special kind of L.A. high as he drove across town to meet her. The scent of sage floated in off the hills…drifted down across the freeways…through the open sunroofs of the Benz and ragtop Mustangs that skimmed along the gleaming ribbons of this sprawling dreamscape.

The low-profile blur of traffic gleamed off the chrome of Harlan's rear-view mirror as he drifted on this sleek sensation. He caught a glimpse of the big sign on the hill…lit up…inviting all those who arrived to dream the dream.

A bitter-sweet smile played at the edge of McCoy's craggy features. He'd been pretty scuffed up by life. But he always seemed to bounce back. From schoolyard bullies to street hoods that plagued his beat to that nasty little scar in his shoulder…he'd developed the resilience of a man who'd made it through half a century…and lived to tell about it. It was hard won turf. But there was a certain sense of warrior pride in knowing that.

* * *

He called it the "Cop's Closet." The dark space in the back of a cop's mind where stuff gets tossed that doesn't quite make sense. A collection of loose ends looking for a match-up with logic. Or things that were just too dark to deal with.

That visit with Slade had turned over a few rocks. And the maggots began crawling around in the back of the closet. For instance, why was Slade playing dumb about Holly's O.D.? A good agent would be on top of that, maybe even feign a tear or two. The trades even had a little buzz about it.

Was Holly that obscure? She'd had some walk-ons according to Lana. Her head shots were all over town. Even a wannabe in a wannabe world has some heat…people she knew. Word would have gotten back to Slade somehow…if only to cross her off his list.

* * *

But Harlan slammed the closet door shut, took a whiff of sweet Southern California sage, and hit the gas. He had something more important on his mind right now. A pair of baby blues that had left him weak in the knees. He knew a little bit about women. And he knew the smart move would have been to ignore the destiny that .38 slug had chosen for him. But smart moves have been known to get trumped by a pair of sexy blue eyes. So he pushed sound judgment from his mind…pressed the gas pedal…and cruised down Sunset to meet her.

12

The Pantages Theater. She insisted their first date be here. It was a landmark of Hollywood's Golden Age. She adored the feel of old world glamour, she said, became rhapsodic about the design…the architecture…all the famous names that had trod the boards. To her it was a shrine. A friend of hers had provided access to the empty theater.

"Like a trip back through time, don't you think?"

Harlan gazed up at the gilded pillars…the rich red brocade of the palatial theater.

"Classic Hollywood," he agreed.

He watched her and marveled at the way she moved among the opulence. She was aware of her looks and at the same time careless. He liked that. That slightly larcenous way her body moved. A bit of Bad Girl inside the Good Girl…trying to go over the wall. But she didn't know that. It was all natural…uncensored…instinct…just like that powder-puff dab she did. It was as if no one had told her she was gorgeous. And if they did, she never believed them. Still humble. How refreshing. Hadn't gone Hollywood *bee-yatch* yet.

* * *

To Harlan the Pantages was a musty old place with a decayed smell. But the old relic of a theater seemed to shimmer in her presence. She brought it all back to life with her vibrance…poured fresh energy into the fossilized history…injecting her warmth into the cold texture of wood and plaster and fabric. Lana was more of a revelation to him than the architecture of the theater.

She smiled, took his hand and led him down the aisle toward the stage.

"Come on. You can feel what it's like to be a star."

He followed her up on the stage. Her friend pushed a button and the immense curtains parted to reveal the silver screen that had flickered with so many legendary screen idols.

She reached out and touched the screen.

"It's a kind of immortality, isn't it?" she marveled.

"Even though you're gone, your image is still up there on that screen for millions to see. You live on forever."

Her Siamese cat eyes danced and dazzled with cut-glass clarity. They were the blue eyes of royalty from some ancient temple in Egypt…regal and removed…notions of entitlement in their journey toward Mecca.

"Maybe some day I'll be up there," she added with a simple, sweet smile.

She opened her purse and pulled out a faded clipping…held it against the screen. It was Lana Turner from an old fan magazine.

"Just like she was."

A spotlight from the projection booth suddenly beamed down...showering her in brilliant white light. She turned...stunned...pleased...seemed to dance in slow-motion as she fluttered like a moth in the light. Then she burst into joyous laughter.

Harlan felt a surge of youth as her laughter rippled across the empty theater. Waves splashing over the hull of a white yacht as it sliced through blue water. Playful bursts of spray shot up...a joy that took delight in just being alive. And it released a swirling wake of happiness behind her that caught him and held him in its swift current.

* * *

Then the laughter stopped abruptly and her eyes turned molten. She became wistful as a child listening to a fairy tale.

"Everyone needs some kind of dream, don't you think? Something that makes you burst into flame?"

Harlan nodded. He had seen that look before. In the eyes of other seekers who had come to Hollywood in search of fame.

"That's what Hollywood is, isn't it...fantasies made real?"

The whirring sound of a projector suddenly kicked in again on the screen inside him. Torn and tattered...misfeeding along the sprockets of his emotions...the flickering image of a young boy in the swirling lights at a high school dance. A young girl's body pressed close to his...only thin fabric between them...her cheek warm against his...lost in the scent of her hair.

As he watched Lana he felt that same surge of warmth...the intense longing he had felt back then. Perhaps she didn't fully comprehend...the way that Harlan did...that a journey over this ground had the power to change you. All the half-remembered terrible beauty of being vulnerable...of engaging in the risky, lost world of desire.

* * *

Yes, Harlan thought. Maybe she would become a star. He pictured her image traveling through the flickering light of the projector…showered onto a screen…filling the darkened theaters and the worshipful faces with her radiance. That human craving to be loved and adored would have the power of seduction over millions of men's hearts. The void inside her would be filled. Her quest to leave that anonymous young girl behind—whoever she may be—would be fulfilled. She would be remembered only as Lana—the glamorous movie star adored by millions.

And he suddenly felt lucky to be standing there next to her.

13

Among the many bottom feeders of Hollywood, the film student was part of a unique caste. They came from across the globe with desperate dreams and bloated egos, to live and work in the shadow of the sign on the hill.

A single vision seemed to drive them all. An Indie film shot on a shoestring that would turn the tide in their fortunes…stun the world with their genius and catapult them into the stature of Orson Welles. But there was something about getting behind a camera that turned acne-faced wannabes into raging Ahabs. They soon developed an arrogance to go along with their vision and began pursuing their Great White Whale with demonic possession. It was a pathology that infected every film class.

Yuri Vasilev was one of them.

* * *

Harlan had followed up on the lead from the Slade case. A Russian film student that sometimes went by "Acey-Deucy," he'd had a couple busts for possession in the past. Could be an accessory in Holly's death. He seemed to be living large for someone on a starving students budget.

Harlan and Azimuth drove over to UCLA and sat in on a festival of student flicks. After a few tedious works featuring headstones and derelicts, Azimuth nudged Harlan.

"This is shit. Wanna go?"

Harlan nodded.

The two were headed out the door when they spotted the Russian.

"There he is."

Vasilev was chatting up some fellow students, nervously munching pistachios. The floor was littered with shells.

Harlan and Azimuth followed him off campus.

"Not hard to tail this guy."

"Maybe we should pick him up for littering."

Vasilev entered one of the run-down apartment units surrounding the campus.

The two stepped inside. It was Friday. The place was jumping with a pool party.

"Do you see him?"

"No."

They began to wade into the crowd when Harlan's pager chirped. He nodded to Eddie.

"We'll have to pick him up later. Got a Code 2."

They returned to the car, heading at a good clip down Wilshire.

Yuri would have to wait.

* * *

When Harlan got back to the precinct that night he had a fresh stack of mug shots on the center of his desk. His weekly ration of sleeze served up on Wanted posters.

"Why can't they get it right?" he moaned.

He scooped them up and tossed them in the IN basket with annoyance.

"I mean…is it *so* hard?"

It was just one more thing that stuck in his craw after 30 years on the force.

14

"Gum?" Lana asked, pulling a packet from her purse.

She looked down and smiled. She was standing on a star of Sandra Dee.

After their Pantages date, Lana's passion for the ghosts of Hollywood led them down the Hollywood Walk of Fame. She had a story to tell about each star they passed.

Harlan grinned.

"Thanks, no."

Her pretty mouth parted with anticipation as she slid a piece of gum from the package.

He watched her as she basked in the warm promise...the romantic vibe of an L.A. moment. Sunny skies, palm trees, an easy laid-back style made it all seem possible to her. It filled her with a kind of crazy confidence that anything could happen. A tap on the shoulder at a chi-chi restaurant. A power-agent jumping out of his Beemer shouting: "We want to make you a star!"

She reverently stooped and brushed her hand across the brass star. Then she looked up…trilled a few words from Broadway:

Look at me
I'm Sandra Dee
Lousy with virginity…

A schoolgirl giggle skated across the playground as she brushed up against him. Harlan was blind-sided. She could have done him right there on the Walk of Fame if she wanted.

She began spouting a list of Sandra Dee trivia. Remarkable, mused Harlan, the minutiae she had stored in her head about Hollywood. But even more remarkable was the erotic way she was working that piece of gum.

His eyes followed her slender fingers as they slipped under the edge of the wrapper…peeling it and tossing it over her shoulder like a stripper's bodice. A glint of foil…shimmering lingerie…revealing the virginal shape of the gum. It rested between her fingertips…full of promise…ready and willing to give up its succulence to her waiting lips…the swirling sensations of her tongue.

The whole ritual played out in slow-motion now as Harlan stood, mesmerized…watching Lana slide the slim shape over white teeth. He could feel the ecstasy beneath those pillow-soft lips…the sweetness bursting against each taste bud. Her eyes fluttered for a brief moment as she absorbed the renegade sensation…then popped open…beveled light striking the surface of the blue Caribbean.

It took only a split second…this banal ritual of unwrapping a stick of gum. But by the time Lana had completed the task of putting it in her mouth, she had endowed it with the searing eroticism of a striptease.

It left Harlan rattled, watching her squeeze that much sexuality out of so simple an act. Thrown up against an electric fence, the current shot through him…fifty-thousand volts. It was a searing lust he hadn't felt in years.

* * *

"Some day I'll have my own star here," Lana enthused. There was conviction in her voice. She looked up at him.

"When you're famous, doors open…people call you. You're *someone*."

Then, for a brief instant, the words took on an edge…a subtle brush with obsession.

Harlan felt an alarm go off. He flashed on all the illusions that sent Holly down this same path. He felt a surge of tenderness for this beauty. He wanted very much to steer her past the shoals that awaited the unsuspecting in these dark waters…the swirling undercurrents that had swallowed up so many.

No one ever stopped to do the math. Thousands of wannabes from across the globe. Film school grads and small town actors and hack writers arriving every year. It was basic arithmetic. Not all of them were going to land jobs in Hollywood. And there was a lot of pain waiting in these streets.

Then, just as suddenly, the edge vanished. And she became an innocent naïf once again. The star-struck fan in Tinseltown.

* * *

Harlan needed to catch his breath.

"How about a cup of coffee," he asked.

"Sure," she nodded.

They stepped into the Gold Star coffee shop.

"Have I seen you in many films?"

Harlan stirred his coffee…tried to lose the erotic image of Lana chewing gum.

"I had a blink-and-you'll-miss-it cameo in *Devil Girl* if you count that."

She laughed with pleasure. It wasn't an ordinary laugh. It was the spontaneous laugh of a child…. buoyed by the authentic joy of being alive. It seemed to burst from deep inside her and lit up her whole face.

"I'll have to buy the video and get your autograph."

"If you can find it."

She reached in her purse, pulled out an 8 x 10 head shot.

"But I'll give you one of these."

She scrawled a quick note on the photo and handed it to Harlan. He read the words:

See you at the movies!
Love, Lana

She had drawn a heart shape around her name.

Harlan looked up, completely taken by her.

"Now I can say *I knew her when*."

Her eyes caught his with a hint of flirtation…as if she knew exactly what she was doing with that gum just moments before. Maybe Sandra Dee wasn't so innocent after all.

"I've been rehearsing for a part in a little theater production. You should come by and see it. I'll get you a ticket if you'd like."

Harlan felt pleased she found him promising enough for a follow-up date.

"I'd like that."

"It's on Santa Monica Boulevard. Opens this Saturday night."

Once again the vision that lured thousands to their Hollywood destiny shimmered with hope in her voice.

"It's an equity waiver theater, so I won't get paid. But that's the way you have to start in this town. When you have an impulse like this…you have to find a way to do it."

Harlan watched with a growing sense of desire as her lips formed the words. He couldn't take his eyes off them. They had the teenage pout of a Brigitte Bardot.

She took a sip of her coffee…smiled at him over the cup.

"Being on a stage…it's a real rush. Do you know that feeling?"

Yes. He knew. He'd seen it in her. That little hint of anarchy. In the simplest of lawless gestures…peeling off a gum wrapper. And he relished the beauty of her parted lips as they swirled over its sugared pleasure.

It was at that moment that Harlan knew the .38 slug hadn't lied. He was in the presence of a unique force in the universe. And he would be a fool to pass up such an experience. No matter what the consequences.

15

She lived on Larrabee, one block from Sunset Boulevard. Perfect for a rising star.

The furnishings were simple. A poster of *Casablanca* decorated one wall.

Lana offered him a glass of wine.

"Sorry. No umbrella drinks."

"Maybe on a beach someday."

Her eyes gave him the once over.

"Maybe."

The wine sent Harlan south of the Mason-Dixon. And the lilt of her southern accent had him rocking on a back porch with some fresh-squeezed lemonade.

"I love your accent."

"South Carolina."

"What was it like there?"

"It had its moments. Something about a 100-degree summer day and watermelon. I could eat a big one all by myself."

She was not only beautiful...she was charming. She was the little girl on the tricycle when he was five...pulling him along in a wagon. Her tiny butt rose in the air as she pumped the pedals...her skirt blown by the wind...revealing her little lace panties that curved tightly across each white cheek. It had provoked some secret sensation in him back then...something delicious and exciting...a promise of warm secrets that lay ahead...somewhere...some day.

And now...here was that little girl...all grown up.

* * *

She gave him a quick recap of her upbringing in Carolina. Almost too good to be true, he thought, with the grandeur of an antebellum novel about it. On the wall she pointed to a framed clipping of a mansion that spoke of the horsey set. It had the inscription: *Falconer Estate.* Prominent in the picture was a pool...deep crystalline blue set in white marble.

"I used to swim a lot."

Her lips paused mid-statement...savoring the purity of the image.

"It always made me feel so clean."

A blue ribbon for *dressage* hung beside the window where a single rhododendron lived...vibrant and green with life.

"Hard to kill a rhododendron," she chirped.

Harlan noticed an open bible on the coffee table. Inside the cover was scrawled a name: *Stormy Tillett.*

She reached over and closed it...ran her hand softly across the white leather binding.

"Another little piece of my past," she smiled.

Then she looked up, a hint of melancholy in her eyes that said far more than she intended.

"It's what keeps me safe," she added confidently.

* * *

As the sun set, deep relaxing shadows formed patterns across the room. They moved slowly to embrace her body. For Harlan, too long living alone, she was a carpet ride of the senses. Warm ambers and muted gold embraced her supple curves with great affection. Lana…and the wine…eased Harlan into a world he had almost forgotten.

An unseasonal rain had swept in off the southern coast to cool down the August heat.

Shards of lightning flashed in the distance. It was a storm off the coast of Mexico. Harlan knew them well. *Chubascos*…kicking up with sudden violence. It sent southern swells into places like Malibu and The Wedge. A rush for L.A. surfers. But they often caught mariners off-guard with dangerous consequences.

* * *

She rose and her lithe body swiveled across the room. She slid open the glass door and stepped out on the balcony…thrust her head up into the downpour and let it wash over her as jagged lightning sheared the sky. A serene smile curved her lips as the purity of warm raindrops poured down over her.

"I love the fury of it," she purred.

The subtle eroticism of her wet body sent a shiver of anticipation through him. There was something about the lush splatter of rain against her skin…streaks of liquid falling from the heavens…crashing zealously…happily…in willing sacrifice…to pleasure this divine creature. She had something that set her apart from the others. A fierce need inside her that struck deep in his loins. Lana was a cop killer...an errant bullet aimed directly at his unprotected heart.

* * *

She stepped back into the room...warm and wet and cleansed by the heavens. The filmy fabric of her blouse clung to her skin...hugged the curve of her breasts...formed a perfect kiss upon hardened nipples.

Harlan could only gaze with wonder and desire at the spontaneity of this beautiful creature.

Then she suddenly leaned down...rolled her eyes up at him.

"Lick the rain from my face," she whispered.

He hit the mat hard...down for the count. Harlan was a stone-cold middle-aged street cop battered by the world of violence. Now his cover was completely blown by this sweet seductress. Inviting him to slide his tongue across her skin...soak up the sweet raindrops that glistened on her silken body.

It had been a long time. Maybe she knew. Maybe she didn't. Knew his judgment was clouded by those killer baby blues. But encrypted in that lure was a deeper message: *Step into the chaos...embrace the madness...feed the inner beast.*

They were words that would plunge him into a sexual abyss like he had never known. An abyss from which he might never emerge.

16

Gently, Harlan leaned down and laced his tongue across the smoothness of her cheek. Her eyes closed...her lips purred with pleasure.

He wanted her...desperately. She took his hand and ran the moistness of her tongue up the entire length of his palm...slow...soft...sensual. Like some depraved snail leaving a shimmering trail of mucous. It sent rapid beatings of Harlan's pulse coursing down between his thighs.

She reached and softly undid the buttons of his shirt. Harlan sat in stunned silence as she slid her hand beneath the fabric...ran it softly across his chest. The same deft touch she had used to peel the wrapper from that gum. Her eyes watched him...full of tease...slightly decadent.

Then she took his hand and pressed it between the warmth of her thighs.

"See, how wet you've made me."

Harlan felt a grenade land in his foxhole. And he willingly

hurled his body across it. Sandra Dee had another side. Something that would give Mrs. Robinson a run for her money.

Long, lean, and beautiful, Lana was every man's dream. A willowy 23-year-old with a firm centerfold body. Raven dark hair. Stunning blue eyes. And a spirit that lived at the edge of a sexual abyss.

* * *

He watched her from across the room as she slipped out of her dress. Flashes of light from the storm raged outside...seemed to gather there for the sole purpose of arousal.

She tumbled into bed beside him...her wet hair nestled up against his chest. The smooth electricity of her body made him giddy with disbelief. But there she was. He was listening to her laughter, feeling her touch, the unaffected way she cuddled beside him...as if she hadn't noticed he was 30 years older.

Her body glistened from the rain. And his tongue moved slowly...lovingly...across the wetness of her smooth abdomen...licking up every succulent drop. But he didn't stop there. He pressed her legs apart and let his tongue glide feather-like over the pink of her shaven pussy. She uttered a slight yelp of pleasure. Then his tongue found her clitoris...swirled and teased its hard throbbing bundle of nerves. She arched with a deep moan and her head dug into the pillow...her mouth agape...eyes squeezed shut...as the sensation shot through her entire body.

"Ooohhhh...that's sooooo gooooood," she whispered.

The moans became unending...traveling from each place he licked. The warmth invaded every nerve ending...sweet with sensation...waves lapping...washing like giddy white foam across the shoreline of her beautiful body.

His kisses fell tenderly...grazing her skin with an adoration that perhaps only a man who has sensed the silken years slipping from his grasp can feel. It rose from somewhere deep inside him.... a desperate place he only now began to sense. These were moments that need to be savored...treasured...because there would be no more.

Her entire body was on fire. Her breathing hard. Her yelps more urgent...aching for release. And then her orgasm began. Softly at first...a sacred vesper whispered inside a cathedral. Then something else entered the cathedral...something more reckless...screams that rose from deep in the swamp.

And with each orgasm she would suddenly go to flame...another burst...and another...released upon the night. The primal sound of those screams...they filled the room...invaded his senses like tons of ice torn from a glacier...crashing into the sea. Then...as quickly as it began...the screaming ceased...rendered into a single petal floating softly into a chasm...waiting for the echo. It was a force bearing no resemblance whatsoever to the smooth velvet logic of a billiard table.

He was dazed by the pure energy of her passion. She was so ignitable. With just a kiss her whole body detonated...an explosion deep in the earth rippling toward the surface. It was pure animal response...from the hunger in her eyes...to the moistness of her lips...to the criminal intent of her tongue across the most sensitive parts of his body. And in her fevered moans shattering the night as she reached orgasm. And then she took him with her...spiraling down through his most primal memory as he watched her shudder and sink into a well of pure ecstasy.

He was overwhelmed...completely taken by surprise. And he loved it. He thought back to those frustrating teen-age days of dating and trying to get laid...listening to the clank of iron gates...the drawbridge rise...an annoying litany of "good girl" rules repeated *ad nauseum*.

Lana was no good girl. Her hunger was pure...intense...driven only by her appetite for pleasure. She had no rules. Beautifully natural and spontaneous. Without a hint of propriety or restraint. What a breath of fresh air. What a manifesto for life. If only he'd known a girl like Lana back then.

* * *

It takes a certain eye to see the miraculous in the commonplace. But drenched in her sweat and gratitude…Harlan felt he had discovered the miraculous. Something told him this was the highest order of deliverance a man of his years was ever going to reach. And that made it all the more precious.

Harlan had known a few women in his day. He'd enjoyed a good roll in the hay to be sure. But until that moment with Lana…this furious combustion of the senses…he was an innocent naïf. He had lived in some sort of limbo.

This beautiful woman was a testament to the senses. From the pleasure derived as he gazed at her…to the skipped heartbeat when he touched the smoothness of her skin. Each time it left him in a kind of stunned disbelief that a young woman like this would lie beside him…and take him on this blissed-out trip to Nirvana.

* * *

They lay there as the moans faded…piercing the silence with only a whisper of what had been. Her body was spent and happy as she nuzzled up against him.

"Do you believe in happy endings?" she whispered.

"I used to believe in Hollywood endings," Harlan responded.

"Then I want to give you a Hollywood ending every day and night."

Harlan leaned and gave her a gentle kiss.

Hooray for Hollywood, he smiled as she curled sleepily into his arms.

There was no going back. Harlan knew that kind of wildness never left you. He knew right then and there his life had changed irrevocably. And if she should abandon him he would be forever devoted to finding another Lana in this world. And there wouldn't be a moment to waste.

17

Harlan set down the valise. Weekly deskwork. He leaned hard on the bathroom sink...gazed in the mirror. A ruined rock-star face stalking grimly into middle age. He glanced at her head-shot taped to the wall.

My God...she was fucking gorgeous.

What did she see in him? What did he possibly have to offer a beautiful young woman like that? What was this doomed, derelict charm he seemed to possess? He leaned in close...squinted at the angular nose...the cynical twist of a mouth...that odd glassy eclipse of an eye. He ran his hand through thinning hair.

He was still standing. Maybe that was it. He was a man who looked like he could hold his ground. Had some hidden secret to survival. Someone who could beat the devil.

There was only one thing that gave him away...that hinted at the craters left by showering asteroids. That occasional twitch and roll of the shoulder.

***

How could anything so blunt and stupid as a bullet have turned his world upside down? He rubbed the burning in his shoulder...contemplated the riddle of colliding destinies. Lethal consequences of being in the wrong place at the wrong time. And the reasons you got there.

Every morning the ugly scar he saw in the mirror reminded him of that day. It was a scar that would not go away...could never heal...because the bullet was still lodged there. He could have the remains of the slug surgically removed. But he chose not to.

It was a reminder of what lay buried inside him...remnants of a species that loves violence. And willing to risk the consequences to get our fix. But unlike the average Joe, Harlan knew the consequences up close and personal.

One consequence was the lighter weapon he carried...a snub-nosed .38 revolver. Most on the force wouldn't touch it. They packed heavy iron. They wanted stopping power...kill power. But for Harlan, a .38 was enough. A well-placed shot could take a man down if necessary...without killing him. It put Harlan's life more at risk. But he was O.K. with that. It was more important to listen to that burning sensation in his shoulder.

Until the moment he felt that violence...that agonizing slug bore into his body...Harlan McCoy had been a man who operated by the code. But as he lay there...like a snake shedding the last remnants of its skin...some ancient force rode riot in him. He felt a meltdown of all the wiring that kept everything in check. What would rise up from the ground just seconds later was something he had never known before...some *thing* crashing through the thin barrier that separates man from his muddy past.

It made it hard to let down his emotional guard and trust

people. He was no longer comfortable in the world of everyday emotion. And his relationships had suffered. It had been a long time since he felt close to a woman. The kind of woman who could really light his fire. That was what struck him about Lana. There was something there that said: Sex is a serious communication form.

She liked to touch. As a cop he had become isolated from that. There was urgency in the way she held his hand or embraced his arm when they were together. She craved the sensation of skin on skin. And it sent a warm message into his brain...and everywhere else.

* * *

Or maybe she liked him because he hadn't gone Hollywood. He was the guy with all his fingers in a leper colony. Could that be what she saw in this weathered cop? An absence of the desperate disease that infected this town...clamoring for the spotlight. Harlan was O.K. with anonymity. He could die totally unknown tomorrow with only a blip in the obits and it would be fine by him.

Harlan stepped back from the mirror. There *was* some kind of substance there. Was she looking for a kindly father image? Good God. She made him feel like a sailor on shore leave. In her apartment he had been like a sweaty iguana racing down the hillside of a teeming jungle.

Some father image.

But as he gazed at the road map his face had become, he could feel the arithmetic of time perform its morbid calculations. He knew the mirror was telling him something else. Something he didn't want to hear.

The glory days are over, it was saying. *The vanishing heat of young flesh. But you don't want to admit it. You don't want to let go of that sweet rush of sex. Because once you do…once you give up and admit defeat to that old man you see in the mirror…you're going to be less…much less…than you were.*

And the mirror was right. Harlan wanted to see her again. He *had* to see her again.

18

The Santa Ana winds were gusting offshore as they drove up the coast toward Santa Barbara. Lana let the wind blow through her long hair in the open window…her bare feet on the dash. Her long skirt ruffled in the breeze, revealing smooth tan thighs. Her eyes were closed…a serene smile on her face.

It was like a shot of Prozac.

"They call it the Montecito Mellows," he murmured.

She uttered a little hum of pleasure. Then looked over at him. There were headlights behind those baby blues…a primal brilliance that flared to life. He'd seen it up close that day in her apartment…like some giant curling tongue of flame leaping off a lusty sun…just as she approached orgasm.

As they drove past Rincon Harlan watched the lineups off the point. It brought back the lazy days of beach-bumming. The primal smell of beachfires. The rush of being inside a perfect curl. The sting of salt spray sandblasting his face.

A slow smile curved his lips.

"Spent a lot of days out there when I was younger."
She squeezed his hand, gave him a high school harlot glance.
"Should I be jealous?"
He smiled.
"Not since I surfed those baby blues of yours."
She was wearing her border town look. Something slightly cheap and trashy just beneath her classic beauty. Harlan couldn't label it, but every time he'd ever crossed that southern border, he knew he was in another world. Dusty streets. Pungent smells. A raw, lawless feel in the air. And nothing brought it out in her like the stirrings of sexual hunger.
"How'd you get to be so sexy?"
"I'm from Carolina. That's just the law there."
"Must have driven more than a few of them Southern boys crazy."
"Southern boys. They like to keep it simple: *You got real nice tits...Wanna go out?*"
She looked over at him with affection.
"You know why I like you?"
"Why?"
"Because most men make me feel hunted. You make me feel safe. Know what I mean?"
Harlan nodded. He liked that.
It was a perilous world. He knew the feeling. In the schoolyard. On the streets. Even more so for a woman.
Her hand reached...touched his.
Then he suddenly felt her nimble fingers reach over...slowly unzip his fly. The way she had undone that stick of gum.
"Us Southern girls like to keep it simple too."
She smiled a bad-girl smile.
"For instance...I'm not wearing any panties."
Her hand reached in. Her confession had the desired effect. His cock was gorged and rigid.

"I'm beginning to think you have a criminal mind."
She smiled with pleasure.
"You've no idea, babe."
She wrapped his cock in her warm fingers, her lips curved with anticipation.
"You don't mind if I corrupt you a little, do you?"
Harlan swallowed hard, trying to stay focused on the road. He glanced down at the full erection her fingers grasped.
"Doesn't look like I mind, does it?"
Her tongue swept sensually across her lips.
"My, what a handsome little devil he is."
Harlan's heart was racing. He gripped the wheel.
"I don't know what comes over me sometimes," she purred as her bedroom eyes swiveled up to his.
"But right now I have this urge to feel your cock in my mouth."
Her head dove into his lap…lips turned feverish and drenched with lust.
Harlan leaned back as the pleasure coiled through his pelvis…up into the primal core of his brain. His mouth dropped open from the jolt of pleasure.
He tried to focus on the road…keep between the lanes…stay normal looking as other drivers rushed by.
Could they see her head bobbing up and down, he wondered. Could they guess that a beautiful woman was sucking his cock right now. Were there any vehicle codes against getting blown at 70 mph? Did he really give a shit?
Right now he was beyond caring. The creamy load was surging out of his balls and up the length of his cock and into her eager mouth. On and on it went…flooding his nerves…gorging his brain…end-of-the-world sounds sputtering from his lips in deep guttural moans.

The rush of crashing waves whispered in the distance. Crisp, cool, transparent tunnels of summer bliss. Sunlight dancing off thin green liquid.

"Um umm," she murmured as the orgasm subsided and she gulped down the last of his load. Harlan lapsed into an incredible sense of peace as her tongue teased the last drops of come from him...licking them off the tip.

A horn blared and Harlan swerved the car back into the lane. He shook his head with disbelief.

Lana looked up with a naughty grin.

"Did you like that, sweetie?"

Harlan uttered some retarded, childlike sound.

"We've probably just broken about fifteen laws."

"You said I have a criminal mind."

* * *

Where did she learn *that?* Harlan wondered. That isn't something you pick up at a Southern Finishing School.

There's an outlaw in there somewhere...ready to kick out the jams.

She had worked her tongue like some bowl of wrestling eels.

"Where'd you learn *that?*" he muttered after his mind cleared.

"Monica Lewinsky," she chimed straight-faced.

He rolled his glazed eyes over at her.

"Well, babe. You've just discovered the secret to world peace."

The wind swirled in...surrounded him with that special lassitude that embraces the Santa Barbara coast. And he felt a deepening affection for this trashy little wannabe with the devastating oral skills.

19

They got a room right on the beach. Lana threw open the window and the salty breeze billowed the curtains.

"It's beautiful," she purred. "I've never been here before."

"You'll love it," Harlan whispered as he slid his hands down her slender arms and kissed her on the back of the neck. Her body shivered with pleasure.

Her eyes spotted the fireplace.

"And a *fireplace*."

She turned and wrapped her arms around his neck.

"Do you know *how much* I love to fuck beside a cozy fire?"

She kissed him passionately. She still had the taste of his come on her lips. Then she drew back, grinned.

"Hope we manage to get out of the room."

* * *

That night they ate on the terrace of a harbor restaurant. A flamenco guitar played softly in the background. The moon danced on the water…lit up her beauty like stage lights. She looked gorgeous. Black strapless gown. Bare shoulders. Dark raven hair. And those searing blue eyes. She was turning heads.

Harlan was feeling proud. Sugar-Daddy with a sweet arm-piece.

"You really look great, Lana. I can't believe…"

She reached out and pressed a finger to his lips.

"No need, McCoy. I'm just a Southern girl, remember? Doing what comes naturally."

"But I like you for your brains," he teased.

"No. You like me for my head," she replied deadpan.

She looked up at him. *Sweet as a Saturday night milkshake*, he mused with a sense of wonder and delight.

"Funny how people come together, huh?"

"How do you mean?"

"Like us. Holly's O.D."

"You're right."

"Poor Holly. But I'm glad you had to question me."

"Me too."

He took a sip of wine.

"But I saw you once before that."

He waited for her reaction. She picked quietly at some lettuce.

"I know. The funeral."

"That *was* you."

"Yes. I was watching you."

"Why?"

"I liked what I saw."

"I was thinking about those eyes of yours all night."

"Really?"

"Uh-huh. Peering from under that black umbrella."

She smiled with satisfaction, ran her tongue across her lips.

"Well, now you can gaze at them up close."

Her mouth strung out the words with a slow, seductive drawl. "All...night...long."

* * *

They were finishing dessert when the candle flame began to bob. A breeze had kicked up across the balcony.

"I think Holly was more than a client."

"In what way?"

"He took her to parties. She made a nice arm piece. I think he got her into drugs."

Harlan put down his fork, took a sip of coffee.

"We're looking into that. It may be why he was murdered."

Lana stiffened, her eyes narrowed.

"He got what was coming to him."

Chubascos. The bay turned choppy with waves. The silver dollar moon melted in the water. Suddenly, there was the rumble of thunder. Black clouds scurried toward them like frightened sheep. Palm trees bent and swayed.

Harlan looked across the table at Lana. Her eyes took on a lewd clarity...a depth of color he had seen when they were locked in the mad dash to orgasm. Her breathing sharpened. She shuddered as if some unseen hand had run slowly down her spine.

The sky split. Rain gushed down in giant pellets. They both watched as other people scurried for shelter inside the restaurant. They sat there...face to face...silent.

"Just like our first time."

Her voice was low...husky...drugged with anticipation.

Then their lips met across the table...a delicious, rain-drenched, open-mouthed kiss. The rain poured over them...thick cream over ripe red fallen fruit.

Then they rose...retreated inside the restaurant and watched as the deluge began. The sky was totally black. The noise deafening. Waiters scurried to bring in tables. And the guitar played on with the eloquence of a monk who had just achieved Nirvana.

20

When they got back to the room, Harlan started to light the fire.

"Let me do it," she insisted.

She knelt down…still wet from the rain…a penitent paying homage to the Gods of fire. Her fingers gripped the slender shape of the match…struck it sharply…and watched its brilliance flare to life. It sent a whiff of pungent sulfur into the air. Lana held it for a long beat…watching blue flame consume the frail wood. Then she plunged it into the dry kindling. It ignited…leapt and consumed the tinder…grew large around the stack of wood.

She stayed kneeled…her eyes transfixed by the flames.

"Something about fire…" she shuddered. "Hasn't changed since we were savages, has it?"

The way she said it…like a junkie shooting up on crystal lady…set off alarms in Harlan's mind.

He watched her kneeling there…caught up in something far more than just blazing logs.

But his thoughts turned to vapor as she rose and kissed him with that sweeping motion of her tongue.

"My little campfire girl," he muttered.

"Mmmm," she purred, her body slowly gyrating against his.

She rubbed up against his hard-on. Her eyes swiveled wickedly.

"I need a fix," she grinned, and laid him back across the bed.

* * *

She knew just how to hit the sweet spot. God, she was good! Both divine and primitive all at once. The act of sucking seemed to feed some deep hunger in her...something missing in her past. Harlan lay there in a state of awe as he watched her...face framed in the light...her tongue performing a lascivious masterpiece. She liked the feeling of his orgasm traveling up from the base of his cock...the deep moans of his trembling body...creamy discharge spewing out in short jolts...gorging her mouth...slick and creamy as it slid down her throat.

She gulped it down with religious fervor. But that was not enough. She kept her mouth there...licked up every last drop with her tongue...smiling and pleased as a cat slurping up a saucer of fresh cream.

Her tongue laced across her mouth...savoring the taste of the sperm...licking it from her lips...smiling with a mixture of little girl glee and religious deliverance at the miracle she had just performed. She looked up at him as if she'd swum the length of the Blue Nile and swallowed gallons of his shimmering sperm.

"Beautiful...," she murmured, her eyes dancing with pleasure as she licked up the last drops. It seemed to empower her in a very primal way. As his cock went deep in her throat it made her feel wanted...needed...gave her control. And now...because of this profound pleasure she gave him he needed her. Needed this. And she knew it.

Harlan was punchdrunk with pleasure. She could rule the world with that mouth. What craving, he wondered, had gone unmet in her past...transformed this simple act of sucking into an obsession that heightened her senses with such passion.

"You're amazing," he muttered.

She smiled...pleased with herself.

"Doesn't every woman do that?"

He ran his hand gently through her hair...marveling at the grace of such moments.

"No, babe. *That* is a special gift only you have."

Her eyes turned dreamy, lost in some childlike candy store.

"I don't know what comes over me," she whispered as the warm fire crackled behind them.

"But it makes me feel so complete. Is that crazy?"

Harlan wrapped his arms around her as she nestled up against him.

"No, Lana. It's the sanest thing I know of in this crazy world."

21

She wanted to know about it.

She slid his revolver from the leather holster that he kept beside the bed…ran her fingers over it in the moonlight with strange fascination. The same erotic caress that aroused his body into a state of insurrection.

"Have you ever killed a man?" she whispered in the darkness. Her candor startled him. She ran the cool tip of the weapon across the scar on his shoulder. Her lips were half parted…silhouetted against the moon.

Harlan looked up at the ceiling, gauging his response. How much should he tell her? But the scar he bore was clearly from some violent encounter. It was a fair question and he knew this dark thing curled up outside his door would not go away. He decided on full disclosure.

"Yes," he answered, waiting for her reaction.

But there was none. She just studied him evenly, mulling over the implications of this admission.

"And...," she replied matter of factly.

She was a cool one, all right.

"And..."

His mind jump-started the horror of that day.

"It was basic instinct. I had no choice."

Her head tilted with a lurid sense of curiosity as she held up the revolver.

"With this?"

Harlan felt a twinge of weirdness divulging this dark zone of his past. But her eyes were blameless and unaccusing.

"It was a time when I believed in causes," he began. "Especially lost causes."

She ran her fingers through his hair.

"I think that's what I like about you."

"What?"

"You can tell a man who believes in lost causes."

The moonlight glistened beautifully from her shoulders.

"It was an act of survival. And it changed everything."

"For good...or bad?"

Harlan didn't want to ruin what they had with dark admissions. Not this soon.

The violent incident had been a moment that could have shaped him in many ways. He tried to shake it. But it hung there...clung to him...haunted him...put him on the run in his dreams. In the tentative way he dealt with people. It was as if this "thing" would rise up in him at any moment...turn on him...or turn him into something the civilized world had little use for. The thin veneer that held it all together would erode. And underneath...a rattler ready to strike.

"Good *and* bad."

He left it at that.

But she wouldn't leave it at that. She studied him intently. Her head turned...gazed at the sky...a marquee with a million sparkling bulbs.

"I knew right away you had some kind of secret."

"How's that?"

"That Ziggy Stardust eye of yours."

"Ziggy Stardust?"

"David Bowie. Damaged like yours. Looks like shattered glass."

She leveled her gaze at him.

"No escaping what we've been through, is there?"

A shadow passed through the room and her mouth twisted with darker consequence.

"Killing someone. That can shape a man. Leave the mark of Cain on him."

This was biblical with her. And she wanted to know more.

"Yes. The mark of Cain."

As she listened to his voice in the darkness, Harlan took her back to that day in the foothills. It was a much younger Harlan then. Before that moment at the edge of the woods Harlan had been a man who said his prayers...obeyed the rules...put his dime in the meter...and waited for the light to change.

His belief that the world was fair and just was still untested. And so he felt safe.

He was wrong.

Something died inside him that day. And he went from altar boy to atheist in one split second.

* * *

Fate can turn on such exquisite detail. The flight path of a single bullet...riding across blue sky...a pearl on velvet. Its smooth shape twisting in a ballet of ancient purpose. For Harlan, it was a voyage to the edge of the universe...taking awareness to a new plateau. Aware of the absence of life...the nothingness that yawns outward...welcoming one to the infinite void.

It was a canned hunt of endangered species. And Harlan belonged to a small group of hunt saboteurs. So he bravely...foolishly...put himself between hunter and quarry.

He heard the crack of gunfire and felt the searing heat of something hard and hot burn into his flesh. The shock of the speeding bullet knocked him to the ground.

For a split second he couldn't believe this was happening to him. His heart was like a kettledrum as he crumpled to the earth. Words that seemed to make no sense at all tumbled from his lips.

His mind was numb with shock...a blackout of reason as blood poured from his shoulder. He was still trying to comprehend the insult of this bullet...the violation of his sovereign being...the disrespect of this blunt and stupid slug for the sacredness of life. He felt a sudden kinship for the animal the hunters were trying to kill.

* * *

He lay there staring up at the sky for what seemed like hours. The light faded and he looked up and saw stars...billions of stars...tiny specks of light...each one a world of its own...all spiraling like a giant Ferris wheel in the sky. And they seemed to collapse and suck him into their massive swirling dance out amongst infinity. And he surrendered himself to that chaos of burning gas and apocalyptic explosions. He was star stuff...hurtling through space at the speed of light.

But instead of hours, it had been only seconds. He looked down and saw a pool of red oozing from his shoulder. He touched it and it was warm. It became the terrible reflection of a man's first fear...that death lurks silently...and everywhere...and always.

I'm going to die, he began muttering. *On this shitty piece of ground. I don't fucking believe it.*

It overwhelmed him. The aloneness of it. The finality of it. The irreversibility of it. Without warning. With no choice of where or when. One moment alive and vital...the next in a pool of your own blood. He was filled with a sense of anger and absurdity. What wrong choices had he made? What passions drove him here? So many unanswered questions. No time left to answer them.

This was it. The taste of ashes filled his mouth. Resentment welled inside him...a resentment so dark and malicious that if he had the power he would decimate the world he was leaving. If he was going to die, he was going to take this odious world with him.

* * *

And then something snapped.

He could have ceased to move...just lain there and died. But Harlan knew the dangers of hugging the mat.

"*Is it hard to quit, pop?*"

"*Not if you're the guy on the mat.*"

The sky lit up bright red.... a bonfire ignited. Anger surged up through his body. A roaring flame devoured all the quaint notions he had been taught about fair play. The gloves were off. There was going to be blood in the streets.

And a new Harlan was born.

* * *

He peeled himself off the ground...crouched on all fours as warm red poured from his shoulder. The sky darkened...and he saw…in the distance…the silhouette of the man still holding the rifle that had brought him down.

He rolled slowly to his feet…crouched animal-like…and lunged forward. He began a slow lurching motion across the ground like a wolf…his eyes glazed…blood pouring from his wound…his mouth open…foaming…fangs bared. A primal moan rose from deep within him. A rumbling growl he had never heard before. And he felt somewhere inside him…this beast rise from the mud…white teeth flashing…a million-year-old killing machine…numb and unknowing…running on pure instinct now…with only one thing on its mind.

And then he broke into a sprint…a flat-out run. He had never moved so fast. He leapt across the ground in giant leaping bounds.

He saw the silhouette of the hunter stand frozen in disbelief…stark terror in his eyes. He turned to flee…

But Harlan was on him…taking him viciously to the ground…snarling with a primal rage…his fists like battering rams. Then he picked up the hunter's rifle and began to savagely beat the man with it. Heavy thuds of the butt against his face…against his body. Bones snapped…blood spurted as the hunter groaned and screamed…frantically trying to ward off the blows.

But he was not dealing with anything of this world. This was a creature from the underworld…a beast leapt down from the parapets of some ancient stone cathedral. Eyes flaring…claws slashing…tearing flesh from this hunter who so thoughtlessly violated a sacred trust. His act was not sport. It was cold-blooded murder. One who could take life so casually with the squeeze of a trigger deserved no quarter…no mercy. And Harlan was exacting his revenge.

Blood spattered across the man's camouflage

uniform…soaking into the cloth until it was bright red. The man slipped into a coma…and went limp.

Harlan's whole body was shaking as he stood over the bloody, lifeless remains. There was no more movement…no more sound. The silence of the forest closed down around him. Death blotted out all but the vague awareness that he had just committed the most brutal act in man's arsenal of brutal acts. He had killed a man.

A low rumbling sound seemed to build vaguely in the distance. He stopped…turned…tried to pin down its origin. Then it struck him. The sound was coming from himself…deep inside him…growling, crude rumblings from some antiquated beast. And to his horror he realized *he* was the beast.

Harlan smashed the rifle over a rock…hurled it down across the body of the hunter.

Then he left the clearing…left the woods…left all the horror of this primal havoc behind him…

Or so he thought…

22

Lana lay atop him…awed by this dark confession of a man who had crossed over into a world that few had known. She ran her hand across the sheen of the gun metal and her eyes followed him with deep fascination. He was a man living outside the law that bound ordinary men. He had an air of danger about him that stirred some kind of groupie in her. He had criminal allure.

"I always found him fascinating."

"Who?"

"Cain."

She fashioned an odd kind of smile. A hint of danger…the suggestion of criminal complicity in its misshapen curve.

"Sometimes I think I come from that bloodline too."

For a fleeting second Harlan felt a shiver race through his body. He said nothing. But it was another dark hint that there was more to Lana behind the sinless blue of those beautiful eyes.

"Were you arrested?" she asked coolly.

"That's the odd part."

"Why?"

"Some time passed before anyone found the body."

Harlan twisted restlessly.

"Scavengers had eaten away the flesh. The verdict was some wounded beast he'd shot attacked and killed him. Case closed."

"So...never tried...or convicted?"

Harlan nodded solemnly.

"Not in any court of law at least."

"What do you mean?"

"Like I said...something like that changes a man."

"Being shot?"

"Being so close to death."

Harlan fell silent as he took the weapon from her, slid it back into the holster.

"That's why I carry this...instead of standard issue."

Harlan's shoulder rolled with a jolt of pain.

Lana leaned her face close to his...hungry for details. Her voice lowered into a knowing whisper.

"It's hard to have secrets, isn't it? Hard to keep it all inside."

Why had he revealed this? Somehow she had become his confessor...sliding the little door open for him to bare his soul.

"Tell me."

His teeth ground as he dug into the corners of his mind.

"Like you said...the mark of Cain."

She nodded darkly.

"Knowing inside is this savage...this rage. And all it takes is the poke of a stick."

"It's in all of us," she said solemnly. There was a new level of maturity in her voice. As if she understood the isolating consequences of his violent act better than he.

Harlan shook his head, eyes shut. But the images were still a clap of thunder echoing in his memory. The snarls of that beast inside him...something from the swamp...from the very beginnings of time.

"It's stuff that keeps coming back. It never fucking goes away."

She took the holster from him, slipped the gun out, aimed it at the mirror.

"Maybe that's why you became a cop."

"What do you mean?"

Her eyes swiveled toward his.

"Is this thing loaded?"

"Not much good if it isn't."

She let the hammer down easy.

"*All* the dark forces aren't out there on the streets. So you became a cop. To control the ugly impulses inside yourself."

He studied her for a long beat.

"You're more dangerous than you look."

She grinned.

"Maybe."

Harlan felt that chilly breath on his neck. The one that always told him to look over his shoulder. It was the black car bearing down at ninety miles an hour.

He needed a tailwind...something to move him past all this. That's what Lana had become. A gust at his back to fill his sails. She picked him up and lifted him out of the path of that car.

She had put him in touch with the experience of renewal...the feeling of physical joy once again. It was the only thing that could quell the beast...the softness of a woman's kiss.

But even as he lay beside her, he felt a lingering sense of melancholy. A kiss could soften the beast, it was true. But there always seemed to be that shadow on the other side of the bedroom door. A brooding menace that exceeds all comprehension. *We humans have a taste too deep for destruction…too blood-thirsty for beauty to flourish for very long.*

It was in him, he knew.

But now the question became…was it also in her?

23

"Every once in awhile you have to double-tap the fuckers."
Eddie Azimuth was on a mission.
They were on the scent of Yuri as they wove the cruiser through traffic.
"Take 'em off at the knees, you know?"
Harlan sipped hot black coffee. He'd heard this rant before. Every rookie got it from Eddie. It was his claim to fame.
"Otherwise they overrun the place. Like vermin. Crawling out of the gutters. Sucking the blood out of the whole fucking city."
"Looking for some ass-kicking today, Eddie?"
Azimuth squinted.
"So what? Watched a little *Dirty Harry* last night. Gets me in the mood."
They spotted Yuri leaving a convenience store. He moved with a swagger from the 'hood and a full arsenal of facial tics as he tossed a trail of pistachio shells down the sidewalk behind him.

"Hey, mister," a kid with a bike chastened him. "That's littering, you know."

"Fuck off, kid," Yuri snarled.

Harlan shook his head.

"This one's a walking police blotter. Let's take him."

Yuri disappeared into a block of buildings. Harlan parked and they tailed him on foot. This time they kept him in sight.

Azimuth took the front door, Harlan covered the back.

Eddie knocked. The lights went off.

"Police. Want to ask you a few questions."

Total silence.

"Vasilev? We know you're in there. Open the door."

Nothing. Then hushed movement in the dark.

Suddenly, the crunch of pistachio shells underfoot broke the silence.

"Shit!"

Banging noises. Scrambling. Windows slamming. The clatter of feet racing down the back stairs.

Harlan took off after him.

The kid was fast, elusive. But Harlan and Azimuth had played this game before. They knew their quarry.

Azimuth put on the squeeze from around the corner. The kid slipped through some buildings, burned up some distance through a parking lot. But drugs take their toll. He was winded. And Harlan wasn't about to slow down...no matter how bagged he got.

The kid hopped a fence, thought he was in the clear. He stepped out into the street. Took a look left, then right. Too late. Harlan was on him, Azimuth close behind. They collared him, cuffed him. Led him back to the apartment to dig up the evidence they needed.

* * *

Harlan shoved a bag of crank at him.
"Who supplies this shit you're pushing?"
Vasilev pulled his outraged citizen card.
"Hey, this ain't Russia. This is America. I got rights!"
Harlan rolled his eyes, stepped back with a weary scowl.
"The kid's got rights, Eddie."
"Fresh off the boat. Bottom-feeding scum washed up on our pristine shores. And he's talking rights."
"That's right! Constitutional rights."
"Just the kind of guy they had in mind when they wrote the Constitution, Harlan."
"Tell us who supplies this shit," Harlan hammered.
"I can't tell you that."
"Why?"
The Kid was snotty, sure that he could beat a couple dumb cops at this game.
"I don't got to tell you nothing. I got rights."
"Well, the man I work for doesn't give a shit."
"Yeah," he snarled. "And who's the man you work for?"
Harlan unholstered his .38 caliber revolver, pressed the cold barrel under Yuri's chin.
Vasilev sobered, eyes wide.
He wasn't expecting this.
Harlan leaned in close.
"My friend here is going to give you a little lesson in civics, Yuri. You see, those rights you're talking about don't mean shit when you fuck with the Big Dog."
Harlan jammed the barrel for emphasis, a hard edge to his voice.
"Are you fucking with the Big Dog, Yuri? Because that starts

pissing people off. People like me and my friend here. And then we don't give a *shit* about your rights. You're just a punk. And in my book the only good punk is a dead punk."

Eddie watched with amusement. It was right out of *Dirty Harry*.

Harlan slowly circled him as he let the civics lesson sink in. Yuri was sweating.

"Looks like the man you work for means business," his voice quavered.

"Thirty-eight caliber's worth."

The Kid took a deep breath, tried to hold in the panic.

"I've never had a problem with that kind of authority," he conceded.

"Good. You'll live longer that way."

"But even if I tell you, it's not going to do you much good."

"Why?"

He nodded toward the desk.

"Check yesterday's news."

Harlan grabbed the paper.

Hollywood Agent's Body Found in Malibu, it blared.

"*That's* the guy?"

"He called himself Marty. That's all I ever knew him by."

Harlan tossed the paper aside.

"Book him, Eddie. I got some calls to make."

"Hey, I didn't do it!" The kid added a bit of Stanislavski to his protest.

"Oscar-winning performance, Yuri," Eddie jibed.

"But it wouldn't be the first time a drug deal soured. And somebody gets snuffed by a punk like you."

They headed toward the cruiser. Outside the kid with the bike watched them lead Yuri away in cuffs.

"I *told* him he shouldn't litter."

24

It was 3:00 in the morning.

"Don't...it hurts!" Her voice was small...shrill...childlike.

Her hands rose up suddenly...like a protective shield. Her body was writhing. Her moans filled the night. She was in the midst of a nightmare.

Startled, Harlan woke up.

She trembled as if something was hidden there...caged and pacing.

Suddenly, she lurched upward with a scream.

"No!"

Her eyes darted...dazed...confused...frightened as she emerged from the nightmare.

She tried to get her bearings...her breath sharp and rapid.

Harlan felt her tremors.

He wrapped his arms around her, tried to comfort her.

"It's O.K.... It's O.K.," he repeated softly.

He felt her trembling as she lay back down. Her breathing

still rapid…sharp…filled with panic…until she drifted back to sleep.

* * *

Harlan wasn't the only one with a dream problem. The angel he knew had been shorn of her wings. Tumbling to earth. Caught up in the brutal journey of mere mortals. Down here on the streets of Hollywood…where all roads lead to Hell.

Somewhere a stubborn and surly secret was hidden in the shadows. Thousands of horrid freeze frames from the past. And he knew how that movie ended.

Harlan held her in his arms as she drifted off to sleep again…wishing he could shield her from the enemies of the imagination.

* * *

"Blackbirds," was all she said the next morning as she sank into a dark cup of coffee. "Sometimes I have nightmares about blackbirds."

Harlan's shoulder rolled nervously. It was too close to his own recurring nightmare. "Why blackbirds?"

"Something stuck in my mind since childhood."

She seemed to want to let it go.

"Hope I didn't freak you out."

"No. Just felt bad for you."

"It's O.K. Just happens sometimes."

She smiled a faint smile.

"Only a flesh wound. You helped a lot. Just being there. Just holding me."

She leaned over and kissed him tenderly.

"So, what's the tour guide have on tap today?"

25

You could fail in any other place in the world and the damage was minimal. But failure to make it in this town sliced deep into the very essence of who you were...why you even existed. Deep emotions had been invested. Deep scars resulted. Self-esteem was on the line.

She wasn't getting roles and he wondered why. She'd invited him to see her in a local play. Harlan drove along a seedy part of Santa Monica Boulevard, looking for the theater. He passed it twice before he saw the sign: *Royal Showcase Theater*. It was squeezed between a pawn shop and a tattoo parlor. A poster outside had Lana's name in fine print.

The place was cramped, tattered, moldy. Held an audience of forty-five, tops. It was painful to watch Lana's performance. He understood immediately why she wasn't getting roles.

He had seen the great ones. There was a reason they were stars. Their faces lit up the screen. Their gestures were filled with nuance. These were actors who could express emotion with nothing but their eyes, lips and the way they held a glass of champagne.

Watching Lana struggle through her lines made Harlan realize good acting happens or doesn't in one split second of magic. You can get ready...prepare...but either you've got it or you don't. Harlan felt saddened as he watched her. She didn't have it. She stood on stage...fragile...vulnerable...a chattel on the auction block...about to be sold into slavery. He was filled with bittersweet pangs of caring for all her mediocrity.

And he felt the anguish...the cruel reality...of why the chute failed to open for so many...why it was so hard to make it in this town.

They were kids playing in traffic. And the hollow, sullen *thumps* of their bodies were left strewn along the boulevards. It was a heart-breaking landscape. And Harlan had to clean up the mess left by all those failed dreams. All the Holly's languishing by the phone with a needle in their arm.

* * *

Waiting for Lana after the play, Harlan hung out with one of the old actors.

"Does much talent get discovered in these little theaters?"

"You mean by the studio crowd?"

There was more than a hint of contempt in his voice.

"I'm *still* waiting for my seven-figure contract," he smirked.

His eyes peered out from beneath a brow dark from disillusion.

"I came to this town in 1946. And I've grown old playing Hamlet here. Still just a poor player who struts and frets his hour upon this fucking equity waiver stage..."

Harlan nodded toward Lana.

"What are the odds she'll ever make it."

The old actor said nothing. He looked over at Lana, took a long, deep drag on a cigarette…blew the smoke at a *No Smoking* sign.

He stubbed the butt into a soggy cup of coffee, his head nodding wearily.

"Sorry, old man. Not in the cards."

* * *

Harlan took her to a small café after the play. She left a message for her agent and set her phone on the table.

"What did you think?"

He had to lie.

"You were good. The play was kind of obscure. But your part I liked."

She twisted her lips, nodded as if she believed him.

But somewhere, bombs were falling. The fractures were splitting the earth beneath her.

"I went to another audition today."

She stirred her coffee listlessly.

"I felt like a phantom."

She sat there…gazing into the glare of a 60-watt bulb…hoping somehow it could be the adoring warmth of a spotlight.

"It was a cattle call. Must have been a thousand of us. For one fucking role! Do you know what that means? It means nine-hundred and ninety-nine of us are going to go home with nothing."

There was a catch in her voice.

"Nothing, Harlan. Complete losers."

Harlan tried to keep it upbeat.

"But that's just one role, Lana. There's lots more."

She didn't seem to hear him. Or maybe didn't want to.

"Do you know the toll that takes on you? So many out there…craving the spotlight. And how many are ever going to make it?"

Harlan felt the heavy pull of gravity all around her. It was more than just doing the arithmetic. More than raw showbiz reality. It had triggered something else. A passion that went that deep…burned so desperately…came from somewhere in the past. Beneath the candy-coated exterior this gently lapsed ingénue was shadow boxing with some old demons.

"The stop-light won't change, Harlan."

Her blue eyes looked up at him imploringly.

"I know why Peg Entwhistle took a dive off that sign."

Her eyes had that look. The agenda of fear. It's what drove this town.

"I'm shit. I'm never going to go anywhere. It's like, if you're not a star, you're nobody."

An end to fear…that's what her quest was all about. As the celluloid rolled through the camera…recorded her image and showered it onto that forty-foot screen…her ego would loom large in the dark. She could be reborn. Millions would now adore her. That was how it worked in her mind, anyway. Her and thousands like her. The silver screen filled the function of love.

"It gets really depressing. I don't know if I can stick it out."

Harlan began hearing the rustle of a breeze…dry leaves skittering across the pavement. A burning sensation caught him in the shoulder. Flashes of a black car skidding in the rain.

He remembered the pronghorns on the plains of Texas. How they would come to a fence and stall. Unlike white-tailed deer, pronghorns didn't know they could jump fences. And so they would circle in confusion…some defect in their mind holding them back. They never knew their own strength. And so they became easy prey for coyotes.

"Everything's not for everybody, Lana. Maybe acting isn't...,"

But he cut himself short. The distress in her eyes was too hard to take. He took a sip of coffee.

"Even winning an Oscar doesn't make people happy. It's just a hunk of metal on the mantle."

"I don't want to be one of the little people, Harlan. The ones stars thank in their acceptance speeches. I want to *be* the star."

He felt for her. But sometimes even fifteen minutes was a lot to ask. You could swing for the fences your whole life. But that didn't mean you were going to knock one out of the park. Sometimes you got it. Sometimes you don't. Damn lucky if you do. The rest...burdened by their mediocrity...just dream...and go mad.

"This town will eat you up if you let it, Lana. It's psychotic. I know. I zip up the body bags."

He didn't want to see her end up like Holly.

"There's a real world out there...beyond the celluloid. Where people go through life without red carpets and flash bulbs and phony stage names."

She leveled a sharp, incisive gaze at him.

"And without killing anyone?"

A chilling edge underscored her words.

Harlan paused...gauged his response. It was below the belt but he kept his cool.

"They take jobs...raise children...and survive as they've always done...quietly...anonymously."

"Yes...but that cozy little domestic life didn't happen for me, Harlan."

Harlan was caught off-guard. This was the first time Lana revealed something more than a white bread past...a genteel Southern upbringing.

"What do you mean?"

She hedged. Regretted the slip.

"Nothing. I'm just upset."

She put on a game face.

"It's just…."

She closed her eyes to shut out the grackles that loomed in her nightmares.

"It's just that…I can't go back. There's no trail of crumbs to follow home, Harlan."

What did she mean by that? They were fairy tale words. But like every fairy tale, there was something dark lurking in the forest.

Harlan ran his hand softly across her cheek.

"Everyone wants a shot at playing God. That's what this town is all about. But the smallest thing you do…"

Her eyes met his as she smiled weakly.

"It's all you need to do if it comes from somewhere inside the real Lana."

"Thanks, babe. I know you believe in me."

She glanced toward her phone sitting silently on the table.

"It's the rest that don't."

She pulled her bible from her purse, ran her hand across the coarse texture of the binding as she clutched it to her chest. There was moisture building in her eyes.

"Thank God I have this."

26

The sleek silhouette caught Harlan's eye. It sat at the curb under a street lamp across from the Starlite. Frozen in time. Whisper quiet. Undertaker black. A vintage '41 Packard that was built like a bank vault.

A shivering sensation shot through his gut. His shoulder lurched. He couldn't believe it. It was a hot night. Maybe he was hallucinating. He shook his head and swilled some coffee. But it was still there.

He left the booth…crossed the street.

Expecting a mirage, he reached and touched it. But it was real. Back when they made them to last. Its sleek black shape rose up from a massive grille, over smooth pontoon fenders, across a long level hood, and merged into its regal-like cowl. It bristled with chrome.

This was a hunk of metal that moved down the road like a freight train. In the muted light the silver grillwork seemed to grin with menace. He circled the black shape…looking for traces of identification. He wanted to know more about this beast. Jotting down the license number, he'd run it later...maybe get a lead.

A hefty man from the café approached him. Puzzled and suspicious.

"Can I help you with something?"

"This car. Yours?"

"Yeah. What of it?"

"Uh...nothing. Just don't see many vintage models like this around."

"Vintage? It's last year's Caddie."

Harlan stood in shock. Glanced at the car. He seemed dazed, confused.

"Are you O.K., buddy?"

"Yeah. Yeah. My mistake."

"You look like you've just seen a ghost."

Harlan rubbed the burning pain in his shoulder. His face was drained.

"Could be."

He wandered back into the café. His hand was shaking as he paid his bill and left.

He didn't sleep well that night.

* * *

The Black Car would not go away. The steel beast hummed through the haze of his mind...careened into the darkness down the highway. And the obscure face of the man at the wheel fought to keep it under control. The rain poured down...the windshield awash in the downpour.

Harlan lay there in the darkness...waiting for a breeze to cool off the baked carcass of a city. But it was August in L.A. A breeze wasn't in the cards. The smart ones had left, but he wasn't one of them. He lay there…trapped and dying…like all the others among the rushing dead whose fate was tied to this tangle of asphalt and concrete. The only relief he could muster from the coffin-like heat was a fan directed over his naked body.

Somewhere…off in the distance…the crack of gunfire. Or maybe it was only his mind playing tricks on him again. The heat did that. It was just a faint *hiss* now…the quiet sizzle of August boiling on the black macadam of the city…barely audible above the *whirr* of the fan.

Then the hiss became more relentless…more annoying…more familiar to Harlan. It was a *whine* now…the distinct whine of a siren carving its way through the cadaver of a city rotting in the sun.

Harlan lay motionless…only a slight flinch of annoyance. Like touching bare wires on a battery cable. It was the warning shot that told him his phone would soon ring…and it would be another long night in L.A.…

* * *

He opened his valise and began the weekly ritual of shuffling through the latest batch of *Most Wanteds*. He had a knack for remembering faces. Things stuck in his head. Once picked up a felon he spotted two months after he'd flipped through the posters.

Slowly he turned over each one…let the image burn into his memory. He couldn't get over how ugly most of them were.

Suddenly, his hand quivered. His face went white…drained of every ounce of blood. It couldn't be! Lana. Right there. Wanted for arson. And Murder One. But the name on the poster read Stormy Tillett.

Harlan gulped. He held it up close. Read all the details. Fugitive from South Carolina. Whereabouts unknown.

He tried to go back to sleep. But it was pointless. He lay there sweating in the August heat. Every nerve on fire. Staring into the darkness as the fan struggled to stir the air and make the night less suffocating.

Harlan had a big problem now. And the Black Car Dream would be coming after him with a vengeance…

27

Too many missing pieces. She was becoming like a criminal investigation. This recurring nightmare of hers...it had roots somewhere in a past she wasn't revealing. But this time he dreaded what he might find.

And the heat of her passion. It went beyond animal lust. It rose molten and despairing from some deep subterranean core. What was the emptiness she was trying to fill?

He began chasing records in South Carolina. But he wasn't finding anything in the social registers she had mentioned. There was a horsey set named Falconer from Greenville. But they never had a daughter.

What he did find was more disturbing.

He ran a search on the name...*Stormy Tillett*. A news article. Tragic explosion and trailer fire in the backwoods of South Carolina. Kizzie and Joe Buck Tillett burned to death. Volatile methamphetamine chemicals were believed to be the source. But no mention of a Stormy Tillett.

***

After his brush with death as a hunt saboteur Harlan secluded himself. He did a lot of reading. Particularly on the things that shaped personalities. It was soon apparent that feelings of power had deep roots in the dynamics of sex. It shaped people's identity's in strange and curious ways.

One paragraph in particular caught his attention:

"I believe the most insidious part of sexual abuse is in the creation of desire in the molested child, the way it forms a shape for desire that can never again be fulfilled, only substituted for and repeated, unless…the person can cease to identify with the molester"

He began to suspect there were layers in Lana's past he knew nothing about. Suspicions that there was no Southern estate. No horse stables. No exclusive schools. And so he pressed his investigation further into the corners of aberrant behavior. The darker shadows of human depravity.

***

She made love as if there were no tomorrow. As if the longing for touch that a child craves had been absent from her infancy. If so, it had been a calamitous loss. And so this hunger in her had festered…and she had become a hot bundle of infantile passions…become the swollen river of lust that now flooded the banks of her voluptuous body.

He could sense the tremors in the desperation of her kisses. Her tongue…like some wet, unruly eel…slid down his throat…seeking the warm depths that would make it feel safe again. Her fingers grasping…clutching…gliding over his body…blue sparks of energy spiraling upward and across and down into her loins. And her eyes would light up like searchlights in the night as the sky split and she succumbed to the bright crimson jolts of orgasm.

And there was something else. The childlike gratification she found in the act of sucking. The comforting oral need that nurtures children in their infancy. It seemed to take on deeper religious implications. She was experiencing an odd sort of communion by swallowing the sacramental fluids of a man…the nourishment from his body. In the viscous white semen was the essence of life…and she would lick up every last drop…smiling with satisfaction as she gulped it down. And she basked in the moans that escaped his lips as she brought him to the peak of orgasm.

And as he watched her there…softly sucking…kneeling between his legs…happy in her ability to serve…to bring such bliss to another…there was a lovely harmony in the roundness of her mouth…the way it embraced his organ…her beautiful face lost in the act of giving and receiving pleasure. He was overcome with tenderness for her. And he felt moved to caress her hair…her forehead…her cheeks…and whisper his adoration.

* * *

In Lana's mind seduction was possession. Once a man had felt the intense pleasure she could provide with her mouth, he was her sexual slave. It validated her existence…confirmed her worth…gave her control of some tiny piece of her destiny. Rejection of her hunger would have been rejection of her very existence.

"I love the fury of it," she had told him. And he understood.

But like an addict, she needed another fix. And Harlan, too, needed that fix. They were becoming junkies…mainlining the pure heroine of their pleasure.

It was borderline for both of them. For Lana, her sexual need had become a psychological strategy for survival. A way to work through some dark horror of her past that still visited her in her dreams. There was tremendous power in such a simple act. Perhaps even the power of God.

For Harlan it was a rebirth. Death was given his walking papers for one more day.

28

The precinct captain called Harlan into his office. He liked Harlan. A squared-away cop. He made the department look good. The captain kept a basket of apples on his desk. He had read up on nutrition. Was trying to bury the tired old cops and donuts routine.

"You doing O.K.? Look a little haggard."

"Didn't get much sleep last night. Bad dream."

"Don't doubt it. That greasy shit you eat down at the Starlite. That's what the perps eat. Gotta eat healthier, Harlan."

He gave his stomach a pat.

"Look at me. Fresh juices. Keeps you trim."

The captain picked up a file.

"This Slade case. How's it going?"

"Still some loose ends, captain. Lot on my plate lately."

"Reason I'm asking…we're getting some flak on this one."

"Why? He was a sleaze-bag tinseltown agent."

"Not sure. But it came from city hall."

"You mean *via* city hall."

"Probably. I'm sure the politicos downtown couldn't give a shit about this guy."

"Who then?"

"I was hoping you could find that out."

Harlan gazed out the window at the teeming traffic below.

"Well, he's not a homeboy. I know that."

Harlan replayed that day in Slade's office, checked a lurch in his shoulder.

"Euro-trash roots. Makes it tougher to trace."

The captain nodded.

"Well, someone has a stake in this case. Wants the file sealed."

Harlan turned, his eyes unwavering.

"I'll play it the way you want, captain. But this is the Land of Oz we're talking. We both know enough to look behind the curtain."

The captain bit into an apple, chewed on it for awhile.

"You're right. This is still our turf. Put some feet to the fire. Get back to me in twenty-four."

"And city hall?"

"I'll keep 'em off your back for awhile."

Harlan turned to leave.

"And Harlan…"

He spun just as an apple sailed toward him.

"Yeah?"

He snapped it out of the air. One-hand.

"Get off that greasy shit, O.K.?"

The captain gave him a thumbs up.

"Remember. Fresh juices."

"Right, captain. I'll check it out."

29

Harlan typed in Slade's profile. The database turned up zip. Strange. Usually NCIC kept tabs on thugs like him.
This can't be good, he thought.
The captain wasn't shucking. Someone was pulling strings.
He'd have to do it the hard way. The way he did before the National Criminal Information Center even existed.

* * *

Harlan had downloaded some files from Slade's computer right after he washed up in the surf. He pulled them out, hoping to connect some dots. He slipped a disk into his computer and hit *Print*. The printer stalled…flashed an error message:

Install A4 paper in tray

Harlan adjusted the tray, hit *Print* again.

No go.

"A4 paper? What the hell is that?"

He put in a call to a 24-hour copy shop.

A squeaky-voiced kid answered.

"Yeah?"

"Hi. Have a computer question for you. Something weird. I have paper in the print tray but it's giving me this error message. Install A4 paper. What's up with that?"

The techie sighed with the impatience reserved for computer illiterates.

"A4. Yeah. Part of the globalization headache. U.S. business has been slow to adapt."

Harlan could hear the kid roll his eyes at having to explain it for the umpteenth time.

"It's a paper size based on the metric system. 8.3 by 11.7 inches instead of the U.S. standard which is 8.5 by 11 inches."

"And that would mean this disk was created for…"

"Europe…maybe Russia."

The Cop Closet swung open. Slade's office. Cyrillic inscription on a sports photo. His arrival in Hollywood with "European credentials." The Yuri connection.

The print shop guy continued dripping with sarcasm.

"Do you want to know about Central European standards for toilet paper size too?"

"No thanks, kid."

* * *

The cue always had a solid smack when it hit the sweet spot. Harlan knew it was a clean bank shot when he heard that sound. And waited with satisfaction for the crisp *plink* of ivory in the corner pocket.

The A4 paper clue had that sound.

During the investigation one of his leads described Slade as half hoodlum, half teddy bear.

Yeah, thought Harlan. *The kind of teddy bear who hangs out with the Angel of Death.* Harlan had a hard time with that whole duality thing. That you could be Santa Claus one day and Jack the Ripper the next. The perps he collared were pretty much the same assholes he'd met in the schoolyard. Just bigger. But now he had the power to bust their ass.

Maybe that's why he became a cop. To get rid of slime balls like Slade. There were too many of them. Schoolyard bullies who grew up still beating up on sweet kids who didn't deserve it. Kids like Lana.

Maybe he could shut down this drug source that Slade and Yuri were running. Get the bad shit off the streets. Keep anymore Malibu Barbies from ending up like Holly.

30

The cool tubes of neon splashed across her naked skin. Languid from the heat, she inhaled slowly on a cigarette...moved only enough to tap the ash off the end. She watched him silently as smoke curled in lazy circles and disappeared into the darkness. The clink of ice in a glass of bourbon had left a Christmas tree look in her eyes.

"Are there moments like that?"

"Moments like what?"

"Forever moments, you know. When you actually make it and see your name on a marquee."

She swirled the bourbon thoughtfully.

"I know what it must feel like. I've had that feeling. When I'm totally immersed in a character. It's like everything ugly inside me just melts away. And I light up like that neon."

She polished off the drink.

"But then the curtain drops. And there you are again. You...and that big empty gutter ball feeling that follows you home."

Harlan knew what she was talking about. The phone wouldn't ring. And she couldn't understand why. He should have spotted it sooner. There was something wrong with her luck. It surrounded her. Followed each contour of her lovely body like a chalk mark on the pavement.

He wanted to tell her, "Yeah, there's such moments."

But he saw it in her eyes…the misery of being obscure in a town full of famous faces.

It was a dangerous thing to wish for because it rarely happened. She might make it. But she also might end up like Holly. And he knew the hard truth would crush her.

So he hedged.

"I don't know, Lana. It's a pretty elusive thing," was all he said.

There was too much shit going on in her head. It left a tremor in her hands and a flutter in her heart that needed fixing real bad. He was seeing Holly all over again. The applause junkies who bet it all on Rich & Famous Central. All the would-be bit players, the bottle blondes…dreamy, desperate Hollywood hopefuls all looking for a star turn…looking to ride celluloid to fame. What drove them here he never understood. Something that had put the chase on them since childhood, he suspected.

* * *

But Harlan had some hang-ups of his own to sort out. He wanted her…desperately. She fed his appetite every night with the best sex he'd ever had. She was the deliverer of extreme joy…insurrection in every smooth centimeter of her skin…alive with a need to be touched…aroused…set ablaze. And he had become imprisoned by this reckless passion of hers.

It was the violence of this wanting that disturbed him most. She was the kind of girl who could get in a man's blood. Make a man take risks. She didn't just open the sexual door...she ripped it off the hinges. She held the promise of rock-star sex in the hunger of her lips...the criminal intent of her tongue across the head of his cock. She *was* the platinum blond that could make men do evil when the *Postman* came calling.

And now that the seduction was complete...she was about to ask him a special favor. Something that would leave him impoverished of his final and most cherished possession...his integrity.

Maybe he'd just run out of character. Been beaten down by too many turf wars on the savanna...too much scar tissue.

He was a middle-aged man, after all, wrestling with his own mortality. And she was a beautiful, desirable young woman. The odds of ever meeting someone like her again were astronomical. By some miracle she had found him attractive...and he wasn't going to let fate deck him again.

He had become a Graham Greene man all the way. Disgusting as it may be, that's how we survive, he told himself. Reptiles feeding off each other. And to his disgust, he discovered he was as low-slung and leathery as the rest of them. That the reptilian mind is immune to plea bargains and quaint notions of morality. It's obsessed with getting what it wants. And what Harlan wanted was Lana.

* * *

When the May-December romance began, it was spurred by needs that neither quite understood. But now it was evident there was something else that drove their passion. Their relationship had more to do with wounds that needed healing...wounds that went deeper than romance. And there were gaping holes of need in both of them.

When he looked into those eyes…those beautiful, beautiful eyes…he knew the pain she was going through…the nightmare that haunted her…the desire for escape. He knew because that Black Car took him on the same ride down Pacific Coast Highway. Every night.

Their bodies demanded this coarse addiction. It was the narcotic they used to blur reality…to unburden the outposts of their pain.

* * *

Eddie had begun to see it. See a cop who had lost the vision…been compromised by his dick. Maybe Eddie was right. Maybe Harlan *had* made a deal with the Devil to satisfy his twisted needs. All the subtle signs of decay began to surface inside him…a patina of neglect…an erosion of purpose. He suddenly felt freighted with need for her. He had become a victim of his own appetite.

And all the time she was smiling that smile that said: *You know you'll be on your knees tomorrow.*

31

"It's dangerous," he protested. "I can't do it."

She was asking for a serious breach of conduct...smuggling small amounts of high-grade coke out of the evidence room. Palming a dime bag on his beat.

"I'll make it worth your while," she purred in that sing-song little girl voice she used when she wanted to get her way. She ran her tongue slowly across her lip to underscore her message.

What began as a healing ground had now become a minefield. She had reached for the brass ring...and missed. No call-backs for weeks. Rejection from agency after agency. And that fucking sign on the hill only taunted her...rubbed failure in her face. She needed victories in her life and had none. Now it was too much. She wanted relief.

It was a strange and destructive dynamic. A textbook case of the conflict and self-loathing created in those drawn into the addict's world. Wanting to help...perhaps out of sympathy. But in the very act of enabling her, he was, in fact, helping destroy her.

There was a sense of ruin in her voice when she asked him. Her eyes spoke eloquently of her desolation. He held her to him...softly stroked her hair...kissed her gently.

"I'm not your friend if I do that, Lana. I'm not helping you. I'm only helping destroy you."

"That's not true. It's my choice. Don't worry. I can control it. Just enough to make the pain go away. I know the difference between a banana bag and a body bag."

Trembling there, her eyes tilted up to his. So needful to escape ghosts that haunted her past. He understood that. Understood the menace of a nightmare you couldn't shake.

"You're the only one who's been kind...who's treated me as more than some discarded piece of trash in this town."

In the best of all possible worlds Harlan would have the will to resist. Good judgment was easy when removed from human need. But a woman like Lana...beautiful...erotic...accessible. The will could bend.

He knew what was at stake. He bore the wounds and scars of surviving half a century. But he had found a new sense of purpose in her passion. She fueled his will to live. She knew this. She knew if she pushed hard enough he would do it for her.

"You like what I do for you, don't you?"

"God, I love it, Lana. You know that."

"Well...?" she smiled seductively.

She had gauged him perfectly...with a woman's keen sense for the corruptibility of men. She sensed what made him tick...each subtle shade of innuendo...right down to the sweet spot that got him off. How did she know him so well?

Then she twisted the knife a little.

"You don't want me to use street junk, do you? And end up like Holly?"

* * *

Harlan had always loved women with wild hearts. It wasn't only her sweetness and beauty that seduced him. It was the stable of wild horses inside her that kicked down the barn door and ran hell-bent for the skyline. It was addiction, pure and simple. Her body was doused in gasoline…matches lit.

But deep down was another force at work. Because of her Harlan began to realize he was at a crossroads. Odds were, there would be no more Lana's in his life. It was a truth he never had to face before.

Just to touch the fineness of her hair…caress the smooth symmetry of her face brought his senses alive. Her sheer beauty had evoked unbidden feelings of tenderness in him. She gave him moments he would never forget.

It had set loose a yearning in him. A yearning for the affirmation of life. And every time he saw the flash of electric blue paradise in her eyes…every time he was hurtling down that rain-slick highway in his dreams…the yearning grew stronger.

He found himself caught somewhere between the saint and the reptile. He'd heard of shortages in the evidence room. It would not be hard to palm a dime bag or two. And he began to think he could beat the system…and live to tell about it.

Eddie felt different. He saw the signs. He knew she was about to take a good man down And he was ready to stop it.

32

"What's this?"

Eddie handed him a book.

"Crime novel. I think you should read it."

"I love the hard-boiled stuff."

"I know."

Harlan glanced at the cover... *The Postman Always Rings Twice*.

"Never read this one. What's it about?"

Eddie's eyes settled on him like a mean fog.

"About a man who gets his dick caught in a wringer."

Harlan figured this for one of his cat and mouse games. He liked to play with people's brains... make them read between the lines.

"Fiction, right?"

"You'd think."

"Where do they get this stuff."

"You tell me."

"What's up, Eddie. What are you trying to tell me?"

"Sometimes life imitates art. And it ain't pretty."

Harlan thumbed through the pages. He could feel the chill of Eddie's gaze.

"Maybe I'll give it a read."

"Do that."

* * *

It was time.

Harlan reached in his pocket, pulled out the poster and unfolded it on the table.

"You don't know the half of it, Eddie."

His voice was drained, burdened by his dilemma.

Eddie studied the poster. He shook his head dismally.

"Christ, Harlan."

"I know. I got a *big* problem."

"Big problem? You're a cop. You got a code. You *know* what you gotta do."

"I used to know, Eddie. Until I met her."

"You're kidding, right?"

Harlan stared silently at the poster. His eyes took on a distant glaze. Eddie didn't like what he was seeing.

"Harlan. Look at me. You gotta turn her in. Murder One. That's big league. They go down no matter what."

Harlan nodded absently. He folded the poster, put it back in his pocket.

"Right. The code. Gotta do the right thing. Don't worry, Eddie. I'll take care of it."

Eddie watched him as he paid his bill and left the café.

He knew women could be trouble. He just didn't know…until now…how easily they could bring a good man to his knees.

33

It was raining as he drove home. She was asking a lot. Bending the rules like that. He had a code. A hard won rep as a good cop. No way he was going to cave. Absolutely. He would tell her tonight.

As he stepped into the dark apartment, a single light snapped on…showered Lana in bright radiance. She lay in ambush…straddling a chair…naked except for a pair of black stiletto heels, a single strand of pearls, and a bright crimson scarf tied to her wrist.

He stood transfixed…still wet from the rain outside…his coat glistening.

Her long hair flowed down over her shoulders. Her head tilted upward and the stark light caught the intense acetylene blue of her eyes. There it was again…that carnal moment…halfway between innocence and perversity.

A faint shudder coiled down through his body.

Her hand rose slowly…curled…invited him to come closer.

Mesmerized by this surreal image, he moved toward her. Her angelic face looked up at him...her mouth half open...eyes drenched with animal hunger.

A single raindrop slipped from the edge of his fedora...fell in slow-motion from the brim and floated downward...shimmering in the purity of white light. As if in a dream her tongue slid magically from between her red lips...caught the raindrop in a perfectly timed motion...savored its sweetness for a sacred moment...then slid back inside her mouth. A vague hint of pleasure curled at the edge of her lips.

He could feel the heat of the focused light as her slim fingers rose to his beltline...parted the raincoat...and deftly unzipped his pants. Her fingers wrapped warmly around the erection she had induced. Her eyes rolled up to his one last time...a sweet young girl...fresh as cream...with an unrepentant lust that set fire to all the quaint, antiquated notions of proper behavior.

There...in that cone of obscene light...her skin glistened with remarkable beauty. Her breasts stood firm and daring...coaxing his touch. The perfect oval of her mouth slid gently over the tip of his cock...soft and fawn-like...her lips pressed down around him. Her tongue a wet butterfly...fluttering beneath the tip...mixing light and shadow as it wove its way through dense rainforest.

He felt the cool orbs of the pearls graze his balls as her lips engulfed him. His head jolted in ecstasy under the white edge of her teeth beneath those pillow-soft lips...then arched backward.... cracked open and poured blue neon upon the night. His mouth agape with the incredible warmth...the unrelenting flowers of ecstasy...the rare exquisite beauty she gave him.

His hand reached...softly stroked her smooth forehead...the texture of her hair. The tenderest of feelings flowed through him...trying to express his gratitude for this act of kindness.

Her tongue was relentless...coaxing him to let go...let go of all the codes and rules and reasons and rage...let go of all the tiny threads woven around the mind like a cocoon...the puppet threads that master us...stifle us...smother us...sever us from the glory of the erotic impulse...

Then...as his body began convulsing...the surge of come coiled upward through his throbbing cock...she swept the silk scarf around it...and watched as the creamy jizz pulsed into the fabric.

Like a slice of pure time sealed in amber a cosmic moment had been burned into memory. It would glisten there forever and he would be eternally grateful to her. She had done that for him.

That's what she counted on. Because Harlan agreed to do it. He no longer cared about the code. Fuck the code. What did it ever get him? A rep as a clean cop. A freak. Well, he was tired of it all. Tired of putting Humpty Dumpty together again. What he needed now was this. The sweet bliss that Lana provided. These fragments of meaning in a meaningless world.

* * *

He raided the evidence room. Palmed samples from the busts he made. If she wanted to get high...dull the pain...he would do that for her. The rewards she gave him erased all the guilt. Life was too short. He wanted her...he wanted this...badly now.

He had been turned deviant by her charms...by her passion. So what. He fed her appetite and she fed his. She fucked him every night with the best sex he'd ever had. And he was losing control. Her mouth gorged itself on every part of his body...bringing him to the brink of religious deliverance. Sucking him dry. His mind. His body. His spirit. And yes...his will to resist.

It used to be a world where he knew the good guys from the bad. Or maybe it was only that way in the movies. But Harlan had fallen somewhere in between…into the gray world of compromise. Where souls were negotiable…and a little *quid pro quo* was how things got done.

He was a middle-aged man, after all, wrestling with his own mortality. And she was a beautiful, desirable young woman. If he was going to end up face-down in the Cornflakes some dreary morning, this was how he wanted it to be.

34

It began small enough. A few ounces from the scene of a bust or the evidence room. Palm it. Slip it in the pocket. Nobody noticed or would even miss it. He was trusted. A good cop who always followed the code. This was a town that lived on powders and pills. There was so much of it. So what if some went missing. And he had access.

She showered him with sexual bonfires every time he brought her a fresh supply. He tried protesting:

"I can't do this any more, Lana. I hate myself for it."

"I know, I know," she sympathized. "I hate it too. Next week. Next week I'm going to give it up. Get clean. I'll check into rehab. I promise."

But "next week" never happened. And she'd beg him to get her some more.

"You like my 'treats,' don't you?" she implored, her voice oozing with sexual promise.

"I always repay you with what you like."

She had him and she knew it. Knew he'd die for one more sweet ride of those lips wrapped around his cock...her tongue swirling...teasing...coaxing him into that blast of ecstasy. Her Caribbean blue eyes smiling as she felt him shudder and unload inside her.

"Uh huh," she would hum as the pleasure began to erupt into her warm eager mouth.

And then that little kicker she had perfected that knocked the jams out from under him even more. She didn't stop when he came. She held on...gulping down the load. But her tongue still worked feverishly...until he jolted again...and sent a new wave of sensation up through his body and into his brain. And she sucked the last remaining fluids from him.

A wave of exhaustion washed over him as he collapsed in absolute surrender to her.

"Feel better?" she would smile as her tongue licked up the last pearl of oozing cream.

But a constant battle raged inside him. Why was he so fucking easy? He hated doing it...but he hated the thought of losing her even more. He was going to tell her "No." *Determined* to say "No." But she had skewed his moral compass with her sheer beauty...and those ice-cream-melting lips of hers. And odds were long he would ever find anyone like her again.

Harlan was a man closer to the end than the beginning. At fifty-three he knew he was lucky to have her. And he knew he was never going to have this opportunity again.

Every time he had that Black Car dream it sank him deeper into visions of his own plunge toward darkness. She was the antidote to this shadow of existential menace that lingered just beyond the door in the next room. And he asked himself: What really matters beyond this? Beyond that beautiful light that bursts from her eyes at the moment of orgasm? She just brought him great happiness. And all other things seemed to pale in comparison.

* * *

If he had never met her it might be different. He would have slogged along his dreary way…never wavered from the code…never bent the rules. But he *had* met her. And it changed everything.

Not many middle-aged men got as lucky as Harlan. And he knew it. Code or no code…this beautiful creature was not something a man could easily let go of.

35

Harlan picked up his phone. It was Eddie.
"Well, are you ready for this? Somebody torched Slade's condo."
"Shit."
"What'd we dig up there?"
"Not enough to make a case."
"Who's doing CSI?"
"Pat Calder."
"She's aces. I'll give her a call."

* * *

Pat was the rock star of CSI. She had a gift for finding fly specks in the pepper.
"We found remnants of an incendiary device…unusual."
"How's that?"
"Didn't think much about it at first. Just looks like a cone they fill up with cotton candy at the carnival."
"What's unusual about that?"

"It was soaked in flammables. But it gets weirder."
She sketched an image of a cone.
"You see, it wasn't machine made. It was hand folded. By an expert too."
"How do you know that?"
"This thing was leak proof."
"So what are you saying?"
"Someone had done this a lot. Reminded me of a *kooljok*."
"A what?"
"*Kooljok*. Hand-folded cones. Still use 'em a lot in Old World markets."

Harlan's pulse began racing. His shoulder snapped with a sharp pain.
"Did you say Old World?"
"Yeah. They don't have standard grocery bags. Just roll up a sheet of paper into a cone and fill it with whatever."
"Any place in particular?"
"I've seen them in St. Petersburg…the Ukraine. Some real works of art."

There was the sharp click of a cue in the back of Harlan's mind. The plush sound of ivory across velvet green.
"And that's what this igniter was made with?"
"Yeah. Quick and dirty."
"Why this though? Kind of half-assed for an arsonist, isn't it?"
"Like I said. Quick and dirty. For someone in a hurry, old habits die hard."

Harlan heaved a sigh of recognition.
"Tell me about it."
He scribbled some notes in his pad.
"So this *kooljok* might be a lead to our arsonist?"
"I'd say. Charred. But still traces of ink. I'm running it through the lab now."

***

As Harlan drove away he looked back at the smoldering remains in the mirror. The ivory balls were rolling across velvet green all right. But the shots weren't clean. They were missing the corner pockets.

There were too many loose ends. Slade, the Euro-trash agent without a past. Ending up with a toe-tag. A gnawing feeling that Yuri was holding back something vital to the case. Pressure from downtown to slam the vault shut. And worst of all, a good cop willing to sell his shield for a piece of ass.

The Black Car would be rolling tonight.

***

Harlan took some side streets to avoid the traffic. As he waited at a red light, he watched a man on the meridian selling oranges to waiting cars. He had the high cheekbones, the soft gaze of a Oaxacan. His wife and child sat at his feet. He was dressed in simple peasant clothing, gazing straight ahead, eyes graced with dignity as he held his bags of oranges like a rendering by Diego Rivera.

Harlan watched the surreal scene through dark glasses, fascinated by the contrast of this man's quiet nobility with the swirl of urban chaos around him.

To anyone else it would be the most humiliating of circumstances. Reduced to selling oranges for practically nothing in the midst of so much abundance. But he held his head high…holding his bags of oranges…at one with some invisible force in the universe…performing a purposeful service to humanity.

It was such a contrast, thought Harlan, to the shrieking

narcissists of Hollywood. Clamoring for attention...demanding deference to their bloated egos...flaunting their grotesque wealth and laying waste to the world around them with their meaningless lives.

What did he have, this humble human...that he was able to exist in the moment...absorbed in the simplicity of selling oranges. Accepting life...without glory...recognition...fame...or riches. Content to just be. It was as if he understood...in the midst of all this bedlam...the immensity of the sky...and the insignificance of human vanity. It was a brief sobering lesson in the struggle to accept one's anonymous place in the farthest reaches of the universe.

The light changed and Harlan drove on. It was only a sliver of time he had witnessed. A mere moment in the maelstrom of L.A. But it set his mind at ease somehow. Stirred the seeds that could save himself and Lana from the ruin that awaited them.

36

Harlan skipped the Starlite. He was beat. What he needed most was sleep. When he got to his place Lana was slumped on the couch...the TV flickering aimlessly. Her bible lay open on her lap.

She had the arm candy look. Her face was a window and he could see a child playing quietly inside. A child playing in traffic.

It was destroying him...seeing her this way. Helpless. All her beauty ravaged by the toxins in her body. Taking away all the laughter. The light in her eyes. It was as if the needle passed through his own skin as well...pumping the poison directly into his heart.

He picked up the remote and clicked off the TV. She didn't seem to notice.

Angrily, he pulled out the poster and unfolded it for her. She stared at the image blankly as the past rose up like a floodtide inside her.

"I know who Lana is. But who is this?"

His finger stabbed the name scrawled in the bible.

Her glazed eyes drifted toward him...glanced at the name *Stormy Tillett* scrawled on the page. There was a long silence as she mulled over the consequences of full disclosure.

"You want to know who I really am?"

Her lip trembled as she turned opaque...a silhouette framed like a paper target in a shooting gallery.

She rose unsteadily...made her way to the image of the grand southern estate on the wall.

"They were the perfect family I always wanted."

Her voice was thin...laced with pain.

"Some place with thoroughbreds...where I could ride away across green hills."

She turned and faced him.

"O.K.... I'll tell you. But the cost is steep. End of the road for the Lana you used to know."

Her eyes challenged him.

"Are you ready for that?

* * *

Harlan looked at the image of this dark creature before him. Did he really want to know? Could he handle the truth of who she was?

When he first saw her she was ice cream soft...lush and sensual...eyes drenched in that lethal mixture of sleep and sex that swept away all his resolve.

But he had to get to the roots of her self-destruction. And as she began to reveal the stark reality of her past, that earlier image of Lana evaporated like mist on a mirror.

***

Spawned in the troglodytic breeding grounds of the backwoods South, Stormy Tillett was found abandoned in a roadside truck stop somewhere in South Carolina.

Kizzie Tillett was a bedraggled, rail-thin figure of a woman with greasy hair and open sores on her arms. She held up a cardboard box with the child bundled in a soiled blanket.

A bony-faced man peered in. His tongue snaked across his lip.

The two exchanged glances…swampland cunning at the back of their eyes.

He spat a wad in the dust.

Joe Buck Tillett put the truck in gear.

"Grab her. Let's go."

"That's where I got my name."

Her fingers ran across the words scrawled in the bible.

"It was the only family I ever knew."

She paused…lost in the gravity of the words she had just spoken.

"They ran a meth lab in the backwoods. *Tweakers*…shooting up most of the time. Didn't take long before they needed money."

The agony of her confession spread like a blood stain on deep white pile carpet.

"Lana…If you don't feel like…"

"No. I want you to know."

"They started selling me for sex real young."

She rubbed her wrists…remnants of cold metal still shackling her to the past.

"Chained me to a bed in their run-down trailer. Screaming didn't help. Not that it mattered. Even the backwoods law came out for his little piece of action. They laced my food with meth at first. Got me stoned so I hardly knew what was going on. Just some ugly man would come in…take off his pants…and stick this thing inside me. He'd grunt…and I'd feel this warm liquid shoot up my pussy."

"Most of 'em were unwashed…toothless…their breath stinking like cheap moonshine…or pork grease. Some got rough."

Her hands twisted themselves nervously.

"At first I soaped and scrubbed myself in my little basin…trying to wash them off me. But I couldn't. And I would cry myself to sleep. Then one day I just went numb."

Her eyes looked up at Harlan…two stones sinking in a dark sea.

"I was broken in."

"I began to have nightmares…this horrid chorus of grackles outside my window. I'd wake up sweating…shaking. But when I looked out the night was quiet. Just crickets. And wind whistling in the pines."

She ran her hand across the smoothness of the blue equestrian ribbon…a fleeting tug of emotion in her voice.

"Do you know what it's like to wake up and realize it's only a dream?"

Harlan nodded.

"Yes…I know."

She stiffened, walked to the kitchen, poured herself a shot of bourbon.

"I think I need something. Want one?"

Harlan closed his eyes…took a whiff of the bourbon. He could taste the warm amber sliding down his throat.

But he knew the consequences. It wouldn't end there.

"No thanks."

She stood by the window…gazed out over the lights of Hollywood…sipping the tawny liquid.

"I hated it. Hated them for what they'd done to me. But I began to notice something. Having men want me made me feel powerful. It gave me a rush. I could get them to bring me things. Small things at first…a bar of soap…a splash of perfume…a pretty dress. One of them gave me a bible."

She ran her hand over the white book on the table.

"That's when I found Jesus. It helped comfort me at night."

"And then I gave them what they wanted. A good fuck. But I realized I didn't even need their bodies grunting on top of me. I could just suck them off. They loved it. And it was a lot easier for me."

"I made 'em wash before I'd suck their cock. Kept a little basin by the bed. I got good. No one could last long in my mouth. My tongue worked every nerve…every trigger…in those throbbing organs. I even got to like the taste of come. Some were nice and creamy. The bigger the load, the better. It was fun to watch them when I had their dicks in my mouth. Like puppets. They would do anything I wanted just to get that jolt…unload their balls of jizz down my throat. And then…after they came…just blobs of jello…shaking…shuddering…completely wasted."

"It was strange…it was like they were transferring all that male power to me each time I swallowed their load."

Her mouth twisted into an odd smile.

"That's when I knew I was the puppet master. And men could be tamed with that little ice cream flick of my tongue."

Lana turned and rolled the bourbon around in the glass.

"The word spread. I was popular…*Teen Queen of Southern Whores*. My keepers were making a bundle. And I had the boys bringing me some pretty nice things too. That's when I came up with my escape plan. Some of those inbreds weren't too crisp, you know. So I got one to make me a key."

Harlan could tell a blizzard of emotion was building inside her.

Resentment. Anger. Humiliation. And revenge. Her voice grew darker.

"I bided my time. Got to know their habits. Joe Buck and Kizzie. Then one night when the old bitch and that asshole were wasted I unlocked my shackles...and slipped out the door."

* * *

Lana polished off the last of her bourbon. She held the glass up to the neon lights of Hollywood playing across the bevels. A drunken swagger curved her lips as the innocent Lana turned vengeful angel.

"And then do you know what I did?"

Harlan felt a shudder coil down his spine. He'd been on the beat a long time. Seen the dark side of Ozzie and Harriet. Children battered...mothers gone mad...the finest linen soaked in blood. He knew even the sweet ones could slip over the edge and he dreaded what was coming.

"I was raised by reptiles. I was the remains of their kill. And before I left I wanted to leave them a goodbye present. I wanted to make sure those memories were avenged. Every last chain and shackle...every slobbering, grunting bit of humiliation I endured while I was bound to that bed."

A low-grade fever was in her eyes now. The same heat Harlan had felt when he rose up off the ground that day...and began his sprint toward the doomed hunter.

"I soaked the trailer with gallons of meth. And lit a match."

Her eyes flickered with the sweet rush of revenge.

"Foosh! The whole place shot up like a torch."

The blue of her eyes turned crimson...a blast furnace thrust open...a bonfire inside.

"And them with it."

Her eyes went crystalline blue again as she leveled her gaze on Harlan.

"Sometimes burning down the house is the only way to warm the soul."

She hurled the blue ribbon and photo in the trash. Her eyes danced a victory dance. Sweet innocence plunging a sword into the heart of oppression.

"You can't believe the intense feeling of release I felt when I watched it all go up in flames."

Harlan sat stunned by this revelation. It was like the crash of a plate in an all-night diner. She had just admitted to cold-blooded murder.

She looked boldly into his eyes.

"We both bear the mark of Cain, you know. Maybe that's why we click."

* * *

Harlan sat in grim silence. Now he understood the complex forces that had shaped her. They had both killed in the heat of passion. To free themselves from schoolyard bullies…from the bewildering oppression that exists for no apparent reason. Done in anger. Done as revenge. Done to strike a blow for softness…for the injustice that the solitary heart must endure. If there were ever to be any justice for these violations…it would have to come, it seemed, from the hands of the violated.

* * *

"Sometimes I still hear those blackbirds screeching in my dreams."

Harlan rolled his shoulder with the pain that never went away.

"That's the problem with being human," he muttered darkly. "The past is never past."

Harlan reached…softly touched her hair. She leaned and pressed herself to his chest. He could feel her shaking against him.

Her childhood had been stolen from her. A time when she should have felt safe and loved. A time when she needed someone to rely on…depend on. She never had that. And now the consequences were clear.

A sense of exhaustion overwhelmed her.

"I'm going to lie down now, Harlan. I feel very tired."

Her eyes had become Holly's. Eyes that look without seeing. The thousand yard stare of battle-fatigued G.I.'s. It was the point when a combatant exceeded his 240 days at the front. When a man had seen too much carnage…would slip over the edge…click off all emotion…become a zombie. When life or death didn't matter much any more.

"When you reach that point," they said, "it's easier to die than to live."

Now he understood her addiction. Her need to mask the pain.

She picked up her bible…held it to her chest.

Her body longed for the sweet oblivion of sleep. And as she curled into bed her eyes looked up at him.

"I'd love to know that you're going to heaven with me some day."

Her voice was the plaintive voice of a small child.

She was one of the beautiful lambs of God and he made a silent vow to himself…

> *No one's going to heaven just yet, Lana. But we're leaving this place. I want you to come with me. Back to where I grew up. Where no one cares if you're famous. And the sky goes on forever.*

37

Harlan met Eddie at the Starlite Café. Fresh donuts. 10-cent coffee. Fading prison tattoos in the corner booth. It had always been a Mickey Spillane kind of hang-out where the good guys mingled with the bad in an uneasy truce.

Eddie fixed his cobra gaze on Harlan. It made him feel like a perp. When Eddie used it on the street you had two choices: Leave quickly…or die.

"This is heads-up information I'm giving you, Harlan."

His voice had a hardball spin on it.

"The brief from downtown is you're on the short list with IA."

Harlan wiped the murky spoon on a napkin, stirred his coffee.

"I went to bat for you Harlan. I told 'em: If this guy's got your back, you have nothing to worry about."

Harlan rolled his shoulder, nodded.

"Thanks Eddie."

Eddie's tone softened.

"But I'm not so sure anymore, Harlan. This piece of trim…"

Eddie shook his head sadly, took a bite of his glazed donut.

"I know the drill, man. I've been there. It's like Monica Lewinsky flashing her panties at Clinton. It's superior firepower. Guys just don't have any defense against that. It's going to take us down every time."

Harlan wasn't really in the mood for a lecture.

"Yeah. Gandhi had the same problem."

"I'm not jerking around here. IA takes this shit seriously."

Harlan looked pensive.

"You've got to pull yourself together, man. Cops thinking with their little heads...that's when shit happens."

He aimed a finger at Harlan's shoulder...pulled the trigger.

"I like women with hash marks too, Harlan...you know that. They've been in some campaigns. Taken a few rounds. Good in the sack."

Eddie leaned forward, a cold fry on the end of his fork.

"But this one's headed for a body bag, Harlan. Dump her. Or you're going down with her."

* * *

Harlan knew it was going to take more than a matchbook under the leg to keep this stool from tilting. He was palming felony-weight cocaine for her. Serious stuff. If they burned him on this, there was no way he could shop a deal.

He watched an old couple leave arm in arm. They shuffled and tottered and it was hard to tell who was holding who up. They both looked ready to topple over into the grave.

"Makes you wonder."

"About what?"

"What it's all about when the check arrives."

He let his gaze wander outside. The sun was just starting to squeeze over the skyline. Something about the layout of L.A.... the inversion layer that locked down the city like a coffin. Thick heat and yellow layers of noxious fumes from a million cars choking the freeways. They called it a basin... the L.A. Basin. Where all the sediment accumulates. Leftover dregs that sink to the bottom. A thick film of scum with all the purity sucked out.

L.A. wasn't known for its mental health. It was toxic to the sanity. People cracked. Did weird stuff. It kept the midnight shift long and grueling. He'd handled it for too many years. But he was younger then... much younger.

Now he felt like he couldn't breathe. He needed to get out... get back to where the air was crisp and fresh and sweet to inhale.

* * *

"What do you suggest, Eddie?"
"Depends. Do you want to be a cop. Or do you want to spend your life checking some junkie into rehabs."
They both sat silent as the noise of dishes and chatter and yelled orders filled the cafe. Smells of greasy bacon and boiling fries cast a permanent pall on every booth.
After awhile Harlan nodded.
"I've got some serious thinking to do, don't I?"
Eddie nodded.
"You're a good cop, Harlan. Old School. We need guys like you on the force."
Harlan paid his bill and left.

* * *

The projector ground to life again. But this time it jammed... seared holes in the thin celluloid.

He was a rabbit on the run...racing across the landscape...plumes of sand walling him in...hot lead laughing at him with that same sick car-door-slam of a sound...*thump!...thump!...thump!...*

He needed a hole to hide in. He needed some kind of oblivion. And he needed it fast.

She loomed in his mind...her beauty hovering on the disturbed air like a single light burning in the window of an old Gothic house. He knew the dangers that awaited him in that house. But he was drawn inevitably...irrevocably...toward that light in the window.

Undone, as always, by the blue oven-heat of her eyes...he kept coming back to the smooth touch...the soft insistence of her lips...

> *You go back, Jack*
> *do it again...*
> *wheels turning round and round...*

He felt like some sad relic in Vegas...eyes aglaze as he yanked the handle. The clatter of the coins...the buzz of the lights...the spinning wheels...it kept him anchored to her. Just one more pull...one more time...and the Ultimate Golden Orgasm would pay off...would release him from his servitude...and he would step away from the game...cease his addiction and be free.

* * *

Kids in the Valley used to get their kicks in the same sick way. Get stoned...stand pressed up against the wall of a tunnel as the train roared by...inches away in the darkness. Inches away from oblivion.

That was the rush she gave him. That mad delirious hit of feeling alive. Until this blue-eyed beauty appeared in his life he only saw images like her in magazines. He wasn't ready for this…the inaccessible woman made accessible. And so she peeled him like a plump and succulent grape.

He was seeing her through a different lens than everyone else…seeing her through the lens of the eternal stakes involved. She was his bridge across the abyss. His need for her warm body was the pure feeling of being alive.

Eddie was right. He was booty blinded. But that's how the reptile mind worked. It didn't give a fuck about the rules.

Harlan needed help. Someone of the cloth.

38

The mausoleum loomed like an ancient Sumerian ziggurat…a block of solid stone that seemed to crush the earth with its massive weight. Cold and forbidding, the dense tons of marble resembled the frigid embrace of death itself. Before it's conversion to a charnel house facilitating the journey of the dead, it had been a cathedral. There were still religious markings carved into the stone. Crosses. Latin inscriptions. Emblems of faith and hope.

The stairs spiraled downward…past two sphinx guardians…into a deep well beneath the crypt. Harlan pressed his hand against cool marble…let it guide him into the dark that lay below.

He rang the buzzer on the door marked *Interment - Authorized Personnel Only*. The door clicked open.

* * *

It was pitch black.
"Hello?"

Nothing. The echo of his voice careened off marble walls into an empty chasm. A sickly odor of formaldehyde and decayed bodies tore at his nostrils.

In the far corner, the faint glow of a cigarette.

"Willis?" he called.

A horrid rasping sound emerged from the darkness. The words were labored…barely audible. Like air hissing from the dry calcified remains of a broken hose.

"Welcome to the catacombs…"

* * *

Harlan stumbled toward the corrosive sound.

"Drop on in and meet your fellow corpses."

The figure in the shadows flicked a switch and a sickly green light lit up the long marble hall lined with crypts.

Harlan could make out the pale features of a man rarely exposed to the light of day. Dark rings circled the eyes. It was a bit of a shock.

Willis sat crossed-legged against the marble wall. He still wore the soiled collar of a priest. A tiny pile of ashes and stubbed cigarettes rose beside him. Harlan watched his boyhood friend with a mixture of pity and revulsion. Years of smoking had left him with throat cancer. An operation for it had gone terribly wrong. Now, like someone had poured acid down his throat, the cancer claimed most of his tongue, soft palate, and epiglottis.

"Mind if I smoke?" he asked dryly.

He blew a misshapen smoke ring into the air. It morphed into something resembling a penis.

"Party trick I learned," he gasped with a deathly smile. "The chicks dig it."

Willis swung an emaciated arm toward the line of corpses waiting to be embalmed.

"Sitting in the dark might seem a little odd. But it helps me feel what it's like. You know...being dead and all."

Harlan remembered Willis from his boyhood years. A young, vibrant priest, tall and straight-backed as a church pew. In those days Willis was the picture of a seasoned Christian warrior...full of ambition and ego...of God battling the Devil. But there were...from time to time...signs of attrition. A fierce struggle against his baser instincts.

Now it was clear who had won the battle for his soul. His pasty skin. His watery eyes. Thinning splotches of hair. The nervous quiver of his hand.

"I heard you quit the order."

"Didn't exactly quit."

His voice sliced the gloom like a razor.

"I was cast out. Like Lucifer from heaven."

He reached up and yanked off the collar, hurled it in the direction of the decayed bodies.

"But the dead don't know the difference. That's what I like about them."

A weary laugh rippled through the silence of the chamber.

"I was looking for a career change anyway."

* * *

He reached under one of the gurney's laden with a waiting corpse, pulled out a bottle of cheap Tokay.

"Even the living need their embalming fluid."

He took a long hard swig, hurled the empty bottle across the room. It shattered...shards of glass tinkled into the reaches of the marble hall.

"How did you track me down?"

"I'm a detective."

"Ah, yes...Harlan McCoy...Junior G-Man I once knew back in scrub brush Texas."

"It took me awhile."

"I'm no longer in the church directory?"

It was the voice of a man that hissed with a contempt that embraced everyone...everything...and all versions of God.

"Been a long time."

"Ever since we were choir boys jonesing to save the world."

He took a long drag on his cigarette.

"So...what brings you to this stretch of Purgatory?"

His head weaved in a drunken haze as he guzzled down more Tokay.

Harlan's voice lowered...turned somber.

"I have a problem. I was hoping you could advise me."

Willis scrutinized him through jaded, debauched eyes.

"I'm out of the confession biz, Harlan. It was too sordid."

"I don't know who else to turn to."

"What kind of problem?"

Harlan moved restlessly among the corpses.

"The same problem you had five years ago."

The ex-priest grunted with laughter. It hissed like sea spray through a blow hole.

"You?"

He held a pathologist's autopsy lamp up to Harlan's face.

"That clean-cut cop I knew back in Texas? Stuck a fork in the toaster, did we?"

Harlan shifted uncomfortably.

"It gets worse, I'm afraid."

He pulled the Wanted poster from his pocket, handed it to Willis. An eerie smile contorted the priest's face.

"You don't really know women until you know sick women, do you?"

Harlan was on the ropes.

"I compromised my code."

Willis shook his head.

"Always the man with the code."

"I'm supplying her with illicit drugs."

"Don't tell me…from drug busts…"

Harlan nodded.

"Even the evidence room."

Willis rolled his eyes wearily along the row of corpses. He plunged a fresh cigarette into his scarred lips, filled his lungs with dark smoke.

"I thought I could do the right thing, Willis. I had choices."

"Choices?"

A coarse laugh ricocheted off the walls of the embalming room. He took mad delight in seeing his friend succumb to the same temptations that had brought him to his knees.

"Do our dicks ever really have a choice?"

Harlan paused…shook his head with exasperation.

"I'm fifty-three for chrissake. She's twenty-five. Absolutely gorgeous. Fantastic body. And her mouth. The incredible nights she gives me. What are the chances I'm ever going to find another woman like that?"

The priest unscrewed the cap from the bottle and took another swig. A cynical smile played at the edge of his lips.

"The *Index Librorum Prohibitorum*."

"What's that?"

"All the things that used to get our knuckles whacked by the nuns."

Harlan grimaced.

"Or, in our case, the *Labia Majorum*."

A sordid laugh twisted the ex-priest's deformed mouth.

"It's serious, Willis. I've compromised all my professional integrity for her. I've sold out for a piece of ass."

Willis rose…motioned Harlan to follow.

"Why don't we take a stroll among the dead and we can lament our fall from grace."

* * *

He lead Harlan among the rows of corpses.

"Look at this one, Harlan. She was beautiful. Even in death…she still has this pale beauty about her."

Harlan watched uneasily as Willis let his hand glide along the pale skin of the corpse.

The priest's cancerous mouth twisted with self-loathing.

"You know what it was that sabotaged me?"

His head shook in disgust.

"You're going to laugh."

"I'm beyond laughing. When it comes to women…none of us are safe."

"Those damn schoolgirl outfits."

Willis still couldn't believe something so casual and seemingly innocent could have led him to ruin.

"Parading past me every fucking day. God, I'm so twisted. That short skirt. The knee socks. Silky fabric showing off their hard little nipples. Christ, they could cut glass! Every day I'd see them. Every day they tortured me."

His face contorted midway between a scream and a prayer. The dark side had won.

"All the prisons a priest is forced to live in! All those years denying myself. Lust eating at me. I was a starving man, Harlan. I couldn't take it anymore."

His voice was tragic as he wrestled with the image of the young innocent that ultimately led to his downfall.

"She was the worst kind for a man like me. A fiery little red-haired bible-thumper. Her name was Clair. She had this beautiful mouth...such sweet full lips. She came to me one day. Said she had this need. Could I help her with it. And then she demonstrated her "need.""

His eyes became distant, his voice forlorn.

"And do you know what her 'need' was? It's not enough that they fuck us into senseless oblivion. Oh no, that's not the worst."

His fingertips caressed the pale blue lips of the corpse.

"The ultimate weapon in their arsenal...the acid trip that will blind us with visions of paradise...that one they save for the apocalyptic blowjob."

He looked up at Harlan.

"Turned out she loved to suck cock. When she took mine between her lips that was my epiphany. I suddenly felt my whole life had been wasted in the priesthood. I had been a prisoner of some medieval lie."

His voice was laced with anger now.

"I'd spent my life praising this Puppetmaster in the sky. And then...Clair. And like some escaped lunatic...I cut the strings. I was free at last. And it felt good, Harlan. The dark side felt good."

His deformed mouth attempted a smile.

"That is what galled them most, I think. The church elders. I was unrepentant. I enjoyed that blowjob. It was like I had found a new God. My *moral failure* they called it. I had embarrassed the body of Christ. But deep inside I felt even Christ would have succumbed to those lips. She was an absolute angel."

***

Willis stared into the hall lined with corpses. His head cocked into the darkness as if he had just discovered some profound truth.

"There must be some special rush they get…from swallowing come. Like communion…"

His eyes lit up at this tiny epiphany.

"Taking the nectar of *His* body."

He breathed a deep sigh.

"Oh, my God…the passion and sweet devotion in the way she did it."

His eyes rolled skyward with the doomed gaze of a man on the gallows.

"I had no brakes, Harlan…no defense against that kind of beauty. And if you asked me a hundred years from now what was more important…my priesthood and belief in God…or that blowjob…I would say: the blowjob."

He retrieved another pint of Tokay from his stash. His voice softened into a warm kind of reverence.

"There's no comparison. Watching her beautiful face…her lips engulf me. That orgasm was the essence of Life. She made me feel so complete with that small act of kindness. And it aroused the most tender feelings for her."

He choked back his emotion.

"*Religion is a defense against religious experiences.* Now I knew what Jung meant."

He twisted his neck to loosen the spine.

"End of career. End of divinity. End of delusion."

He looked up with a sappy grin.

"I feel much better now."

Harlan shook his head in sad recognition.

"Yes. Exactly. That's what I'm battling."

"Well, my friend, if that's the case then grab an oar and we'll row across the River Styx together."

Harlan became more desperate.

"God, Willis, I was hoping for a little more tangible advice."

"Take a gander, Harlan. Does this look like a man who has found the answers?"

Harlan looked at the pathetic figure shrouded in the green light of the mausoleum. Pasty skin. Rheumy eyes. Trembling hands. Marooned in a mist of cheap Tokay. All the once bright purpose corrupted by appetite.

He knew he was on his own. He returned back to the light of day, leaving Willis to accompany the dead on their final voyage into eternity.

39

When Harlan returned home she was strung out on the couch in a tattered bathrobe. Her self-neglect tortured him.

She looked up, smiled weakly.

"I need a bath," she said quietly, almost as a plea.

He helped her stumble to the tub.

The robe fell to the floor and Lana slipped into the warm water and lay back with her eyes closed. There was healing in the feel of naked skin immersed in liquid. If gulping sperm was a form of communion for her, then the bath was a purification ceremony.

It was welcome escape from all her failings…a way to cleanse herself emotionally.

Harlan kneeled beside the tub and began soaping her body. It surprised him how intimately he knew every detail. Her physical beauty was a credit to the species. The satin smoothness of her skin. The shape of her breasts. The firmness of her thighs. The way her belly curved down to her pudenda. The slenderness of her arms and delicate bones in her hands.

He cupped the warm water like a priest absolving her...let it flow over her body to wash away the sin. He tilted up her head and she accepted the blessings of the liquid as it washed through her hair and over her face.

It was a small moment. But for her it was a ritual purging of the past. Of all the horrors that she had endured. She had become so vulnerable in the world...the maddening failure of her quest...the pain that would not end...that she would reach out and give herself to anyone who showed a bit of kindness. Harlan felt overcome by a moment of tenderness for her...glad to be the one offering that solace. He wished somehow he could protect her from the assaults of a vicious world as he leaned down and kissed her gently on the forehead. Her lips curved into a weak smile.

"I appreciate everything you do for me."

Some old song played through his head as he anointed her with the healing waters. He sang it softly to her:

*You don't have to be
a star, baby,
to be in my show...*

He dried her with a towel and lay her down in bed. Then he curled up beside her and held her close to him as she fell asleep.

* * *

As he lay there gazing into the darkness, images of Holly played through his mind. Wheeling her out on a gurney at 3 a.m. Blue arm dangling from under the sheet. Skin full of needle marks. The silver bracelet hung loosely on her wrist. The word *Holly* engraved on it.

It was that vague, distant, surreal stare in Holly's dead eyes that got him the most. The dream that died...the spirit that curled into a ball...long before the last needle nailed her to the everlasting night.

He wanted to read Holly her rights that night...

> *You have the right to get out of this shithole before it's too late. Before it eats your heart and corrodes your soul. Before all the delusions of that sign on the hill snuff the one and only life you'll ever know...*

But Hollywood was never fussy about reading Miranda rights. Especially to wannabes like Holly. And all the others just like her who arrived by the busload every day. They called it *The Perfect Illusion*. And when the seduction was complete, it required a spectacular denial system. A drug. A drink. A needle in the arm. Whatever it took to cling to the illusion of becoming a star.

And then...one night...the dream was over. Never going to happen. Just another loser in Losertown.

That's when Harlan's phone rang. And he watched all the terrible things that the suffocation of the spirit can do to people...the parade of blue arms wheeled out through the night. They said no one leaves Hollywood unless they find God. But sometimes God comes in the guise of a hypodermic.

He feared for her future as he curled up beside Lana. He wrapped his arms around her...felt her warm body and soft breathing as he drifted off to sleep.

40

Harlan watched the car pull up across the street. Slip under a silky veil of light from a street lamp. It draped the huge steel shape in menacing shadow. He squinted. A jolt of panic turned his stomach into knots. He tried to steady his hand as he took a swig of coffee.

Was he going crazy? It was dark, but he was sure that was the car. The '41 Packard in his dream. Big bold headlights. Silver grillwork. Solid steel. Doomsday black.

A heavy-set man emerged from the car...strode toward the café. Harlan watched him as he crossed the street and entered. He paused in the harsh fluorescent light and surveyed the late night crowd. His eyes sized up each one like a pro. Who was a potential threat and who was an ally if things got ugly. Harlan knew right away this guy was a cop. But nobody local.

The man headed straight toward Harlan's booth.

Harlan felt his pulse race. His shoulder snap. He opened his jacket...weapon at the ready.

The man bore down on him...rolling his weight with a slow side-to-side motion like he was negotiating the deck of a ship at sea.

As he got closer Harlan computed the details. Worn leather boots. Pale skin. Jowly moon face. Deep-set eyes. Thick hands. And under his coat...the tell-tale bulge of a weapon. Not just any weapon...a real ego-piece.

Harlan's back went up. Outwardly he stayed cool. But inside he was a coiled viper.

The man stopped at Harlan's booth. He rolled a toothpick across his lip.

"You Harlan McCoy?"

Harlan slid his eyes up slow and easy. Never let 'em see you sweat. The man's belly hung over his belt at eye level. Must be rural. Never make it as an L.A. cop.

"Could be. Who's asking?"

The man slipped a brass star from his pocket.

"Earl Duke. Greenville County Sheriff's Department."

"Greenville?"

His head bobbed, annoyed at having to explain.

"South Carolina."

The words hit Harlan like a wrecking ball. He toyed with a fry to keep from blowing his cover.

"Long way from home. Looking for a job out here?"

"Looking for a fugitive."

The man tossed a manila envelope on the table.

"Mind if I join you?"

Harlan's mind was racing. This could only end badly.

Reluctantly, he nodded to the empty seat. The man squeezed his bulk into the booth.

"Been doing some police-work on a case. Brought me out to L.A. Sort of a busman's holiday."

An Ahab cop. Obsessed with a white whale 24/7. Just what Harlan needed.

"What case?"

The man opened the envelope...pulled out a dog-eared packet. Clipped to the top sheet was a photo.

Harlan felt his heart sink.

"Arson. Two people died in a meth lab explosion."

His stubby finger landed on the photo like a bayonet.

"That makes it Murder One where I come from."

There was a cold, merciless edge to his voice.

"Meth is a dangerous business. Volatile stuff. Dealers blow themselves up all the time."

"True. Except for one thing."

"What's that?"

"There should have been three bodies in that fire."

"The perp."

"Yeah. This Joe Buck. I knew him. Tough as beaver hide. Even while he was dying he had enough grit to leave a clue."

"What was that?"

"Scrawled a name in the soot."

He looked up, snapped the toothpick off in his teeth.

"Stormy."

His finger stabbed the photo once again.

"Her."

Harlan felt his shoulder begin to lurch. He covered it reaching for his coffee.

"She looks kind of innocent to me. Think this Joe Buck had an agenda?"

"Innocent? That little swamp bitch was a copperhead."

"You seem to know her pretty well."

His eyes went dark and distant...something there in the shadows.

"Yeah…I know her."

He swiveled back into the fluorescent glare of the Starlite.

"Got a warrant to pick her up. Heard you might know her whereabouts."

His cop eyes fixed menacingly on Harlan.

"Maybe doing porn now."

Some people deserve to die. Harlan knew instinctively this missing link was one of them. A bully out of his schoolyard past. Harlan's impulse was to plant the cold blue steel of his .38 right between the guy's beady eyes right now. Pull the trigger. Blam. Twice. Save the world a lot of grief.

"Who told you I knew her?"

The man had been sniffing the sweet aroma of Harlan's plate of fries. He needed a grease fix.

"Mind?"

Harlan pushed the plate of saturated fat across the table.

"Knock yourself out."

He watched with a sense of revulsion as the man stuffed handfuls of the greasy sticks into his mouth.

"You were working some O.D. case, right? They ran in the same circles."

Good. He didn't seem to know the extent of his connection to Lana.

"Still working that one. This is L.A. Stretched thin."

The man nodded. The fries were disappearing fast.

Maybe his arteries will seize up right now, Harlan was hoping. *Get this bloodhound off the scent.*

Harlan reached for the photo.

"But I can keep this photo with me," he offered. "Help me I.D. her."

A greasy finger snapped down…pinned it to the table.

"Uh uh. Only one I got."

Worth a shot. Now the photo at least had a big blob of grease on it.

Harlan picked up his tab, began to leave.

"Been a long night. Need some sack time. Good luck with your fugitive."

The man gave him the cop's once over. It was ripe with subtext. A moment of backwoods cunning versus big city street smarts.

"You'll keep me in the loop then, right?"

"Right."

Harlan took a step, paused, turned.

"That your old Packard out there?"

"Packard? Those went out with Dillinger."

Harlan couldn't hide the twitch in his shoulder. Earl mulled over its significance as he picked his teeth.

"Drive a Lincoln. Ain't that old. Why?"

Harlan peered into the darkness outside. His mind was screwing with him.

"Nothing."

* * *

As he headed down the 405 Harlan was already forming an exit strategy. He knew what he had to do now. It was now or never. The hounds were on the scent. It was the only choice left. He had to get Lana out of here fast. And screw the consequences.

41

He never could tolerate dirty cops. Now he was one. And it haunted him.

How did he ever get into this mess?

Two baby blues beneath a black umbrella. That's how.

What was it that drove this obsession he couldn't shake...no matter the cost. Under her influence he had become capable of criminal acts. And it had opened the door to ruin.

His whole life had been played clean. Straight. By the book. Crisp shots that put the ball in the pocket with just a touch of English. Now it was all unraveling. Bank shots spinning wildly out of control.

How could she have such a powerful hold on him? It was the force of some other self at work. Something dark and decadent and primal that lives only for gratification. And the soul would have to work out the price that must be paid.

***

He *could* become righteous and drive her away. Or he could accept his role as accessory…and spend his nights languishing in her gratitude…and deal with the guilt later.

The problem was…a man of 53 has limited choices. The days of sexual abundance are past. Most young women looked right through him. He had become invisible to them. All but Lana.

And there were other forces at work. She was sweet. She was charming. Everything about her enslaved his senses. She had a soft beauty that men craved. He saw it in their eyes…just to be in her presence…to feel the thrill that sprang from each movement of her body…each flicker of invitation in her eyes…each glistening ray of sun that warmed her shoulders. He watched it weaken other men. They were envious of him. He had made every attempt to resist her. But reason was quickly turned into abandon. He was undone…just as Willis had been…and left to her devices without the will to resist.

What made her even more dangerous was that not every woman could do this. Most others simply had no allure for him. They were wax fruit. No real juice when you bit into them.

And that's why he was unwilling to relinquish her. When would he ever have another opportunity for this slice of heaven?

But like a skipping stone…breaking the calm surface of the pond…it was all unraveling now. Internal Affairs breathing down his neck. That bloodhound sheriff on the scent. The silent assassin inside Lana's head. And the Black Car dream. It was the last thing he heard every night. The horrible fleshy sound of a human body smashing against a car windshield. It was turning him into a freakin' basket case.

* * *

Stormy Tillett had taken the name Lana in tribute to one of her favorite stars. She believed it would redefine her destiny. It had a nice ring to it. Hot platinum blond...sultry femme fatale...smoking handgun aimed at the cad who had just done his last bad deed. And maybe that cad turned out to be Byron Slade.

Harlan kept playing with it...trying not to believe it. But it kept pushing back into his mind. Maybe she *had* made the hit on Slade. Lana had plenty of buttons. Just push the right button. And this time she wasn't chained to a bed.

"I was there that night," she admitted when he pressed her. "He promised me a role."

"But it was just a cheap casting couch ploy. He put the make on me. I said 'No.' He got rough and I left."

Her face was stone-cold...unapologetic.

"I would like to have killed him. He was a pig. But someone else did the world that favor."

But who then? Who else had enough reason to kill him? Sure, Slade had plenty of professional enemies in this town. It was the Hollywood Code. Trample the weak. Hurdle the dead. But that was part of the hardball game in *The Industry.*

Harlan couldn't bring himself to face the truth that she might have done it. He needed her. And for desperate reasons of his own he left her mask intact...let the sanctity of her word go undisturbed. And so he became the dirty cop...telling lies to himself...breaking his code...yielding to criminal acts...in order to experience the splendor of her touch.

He hated himself for it, but his failings were not unlike those that plagued much of humanity. And despite his corruption,

Harlan began to see a core of personal truth in her that could save her. He began devising an exit strategy that might make all their demons go away.

At least for awhile.

42

"He was a perv. What can I tell you?"

Yuri could set things right. He was key to nailing the case. But he was slippery. They were going to have to mess with this guy's reality. Under pressure of getting deported he began to rethink his story. Even U.S. jail time looked better than going back to frigid winters and bread lines.

"You know what I like about this country?"

"Stick to the point."

"Warm showers. I love a warm shower in the morning. People stink where I'm from."

Harlan tapped the photo of Slade's dead body that was on the table. Oscar and all.

"Tell us about it, Yuri. Or you're on the next boat out. No more of this *perestroika* shit."

As Harlan suspected, the weasel knew a lot more about Slade than he'd first let on.

"He liked to party. Had a game he played."

"A game?"

"You know. Clinton? The cigar?"

"Yeah."

"Well, Slade had his own version. Turned on certain types of women."

"What type is that?"

"The Hollywood wannabe."

Yuri saw where this was going and he began to squirm.

"Look, I feel bad about Holly. But I didn't give her the bad junk. Maybe she knew something that made her a risk. Slade was seeing her. He was seeing lots of 'em. That was his game plan. Promise 'em a role in some shitty flick and they'd drop their pants. I guess they got a rush from that little bald head in their slots."

He leaned back…tried for a game face with a cynical toss of the head.

"But that was the closest they were ever going to get to one."

The dots were starting to connect. Did Slade have something to hide that Holly could compromise? Was that why she was killed? And was Slade's murder an act of revenge for Holly's death? It was beginning to look that way…and Harlan didn't like it.

* * *

The projector kicked to life. Celluloid cranking at 24-frames-per-second. Forget *Gidget*. This was *Madame X*. Harlan played with the possibilities. Lana with a smoking gun. If Lana *had* done it here's how it was scripted:

No signs of a struggle. It must have been someone he knew. Lana was there that night. Like she said, as a client. A drink. Slade gets her stoned on high-grade coke. Promises her a role if she'll "polish his Oscar." He holds the statue at waist level.

"Lets see what you can do for the camera."

Desperate for the limelight, and knowing Slade had the power to make it happen, Lana drops to her knees. She engulfs the smooth, round head of the golden statue in her mouth.

"Ohh, I think you've got the talent I'm looking for."

Slade runs the smooth head of the statue up her thighs...over her pussy. He peels off her panties...tosses them into the sea below. They float on the wind...soft lace swirling on currents of air...

But then he makes a fatal error. He gets rough. And he unleashes demons he had no idea existed. A savagery stored inside her since childhood that would rise up and devour him.

Flashes of her subjugation in the backwoods of Carolina explode in her head...chained and helpless...rednecks spewing their spunk on her. Her fear turns to rage. In a fit of vengeance...for Holly's death...for her own degradation...she grabs the Oscar and clubs him. He slumps over the railing, unconscious. She angrily shoves the Oscar up his ass, dumps his nude body over the railing into the sea.

It was a bizarre, but valid scenario. Harlan took a deep breath. He didn't want to believe it...even with all he knew about her. But if it wasn't Lana, then who?

Harlan took another tack. *We Know Everything. You might as well confess.*

"You had the best shot at him, Yuri. Why'd you pole-axe him?"

Eddie chimed in.

"We mean...other than ridding the world of assholes."

Yuri was sweating now.

"I *didn't* do it. I swear. Why would I? He was my ticket to the Big Time."

"What do you mean?"

"I'm a fucking film student. Bottom of the barrel. He was going to be my *Citizen Kane*."

Harlan and Eddie looked at each other.

"How's that?"

Yuri hedged.

"Well, he just had some interesting history, O.K.?"

"Interesting?"

"Yeah. There was a lot more to this guy than pinky rings and shark-skin suits. I was writing a script about him."

Harlan gave Eddie a look. In the wrong hands that script might be what got Slade killed. And why the condo was torched.

"And this killer script…where is it?"

"I gave it to him. To get his input. Then the dickhead went and got himself murdered."

He added a final disclaimer.

"But it *wasn't* me. O.K.?"

43

Before he could sort it all out…get a grip on things…Harlan got a call. A doctor at the Angel of Mercy Institute. It was a catholic hospital for the mentally ill.

"Willis asked me to call you."

"He's in trouble?"

"I'm afraid so. There was…an incident."

When Harlan arrived they led him to a private room.

"He's been classified fifty-one-fifty. That's why he's confined."

Fifty-one-fifty. A danger to himself or others. Willis had gone over the edge. Should have seen it coming.

A beefy orderly unlocked the door for Harlan to enter.

"Knock when you want to leave."

The ex-priest looked up from the bed.

"What'd you do, Willis? Why are you here?"

His expression was anguished. His voice hoarse…rasping that hissing sound…like walking over crushed gravel.

"She was beautiful, Harlan. Lying there…"

The torture of his voice rose from needs deep inside…needs that had gone unmet for too many years.

"Even in death…she had this pale beauty about her…"

His face winced with pain.

"I…I couldn't help myself."

The billion-year-old force inside him would not be denied.

His head hung in humiliation.

"I fucked her, Harlan. I fucked the corpse."

Harlan went blank. He stood immobile for a long beat…trying to deal with the image.

"You actually…"

"Yes."

Harlan shook his head. He was a cop. He'd seen it all. But this was a new one. And this was Willis…the sweet kid he grew up with.

Anger suddenly curled up inside the former priest…thick as smoke from a doused fire.

"Why did I become a priest? Why was I so blind? Denying myself all those incredible feelings of being alive?"

He stood and gripped the bars on the window…his voice a ripsaw slicing through dry logs.

"They're keeping me here awhile. Extreme makeover from the shrinks."

His eyes narrowed…his voice acidic.

"Evidently fucking dead bodies is considered aberrant behavior."

Harlan shook his head wearily.

"You said you might have something for me."

Willis sighed.

"Yeah. I got to thinking…lot of time for that in here. Remembered what you said about the agent's office. Strong odor of garlic."

Harlan took out his notebook, scribbled some words.

"One stiff I worked on. A real mess. Could hardly recognize the guy. Whacked by some underworld thugs. But he still had this strong smell of garlic about him."

Willis shuffled around the room in an old pair of shoes.

"You know, they eat that stuff like candy in the Old World. This guy was from the Ukraine."

He looked around, agitated.

"Damn! I wish they'd let us smoke in here."

He turned to Harlan.

"Where was I?"

"Garlic smell."

"Oh yeah. But here's the kicker. Found out this thug was in the Witness Protection Program. Somehow his past caught up with him. Got whacked by some KGB gone free-lance after the fall."

Willis was edgy. He kept looking toward the door.

"The point is…they give 'em a new identity. But old habits die hard. This guy had to have his fix of garlic. Could be how they tracked him."

Harlan mulled it over. It made sense. The stench he'd picked up in Slade's office that day. It was garlic oozing out of the guy's skin. Other pieces began to fit. The Cyrillic scrawl on a sports photo. A4 paper. The kooljok used to torch the condo. Maybe Slade wasn't Slade after all.

* * *

The beefy orderly approached Willis's room…knocked.

"Time's up."

Willis shuddered…eyes filled with panic.

"Get me out of here, Harlan. You've got to get me out of here."

Harlan could feel his pain, but what could he do. Willis had taken a wrong turn…gotten busted for perversion. Now he was locked down in an institution that saw him as a lab rat.

The door swung open. Willis saw his chance. He bolted past the orderly, raced down the corridor. The orderly took off after him, sounding the alarm. Willis had barely reached the end of the hall when two more white coats tackled him. Harlan watched in horror as the ex-priest struggled ferociously. He was surprised by the strength of his resistance. But five muscled orderlies were now on him, pinning his limbs and head to the floor. His eyes turned dark and forlorn as all hope faded. His struggle was futile.

A doctor calmly walked over, slammed a hypodermic in his arm. He turned to Harlan.

"Sorry you had to see that. Five point take down. It's the only way."

Harlan stood helplessly…watched as his friend's body slowly went limp. The orderlies removed his shoelaces…carried him back to his room.

As they passed, Willis looked up, his eyes wild, half-mad.

"Look…no shoe laces. Afraid I might hang myself with 'em."

Nervous laughter spilled from his upturned face.

"Are they kidding? I'm a priest. I have God! Only someone who's lost all hope…who's life is empty of meaning would do that."

44

The next day Harlan put in a call to an agent at the Bureau. Harlan identified himself, explained the developments in the case.

There was a long silence.

"I can't discuss this on the phone. Can we meet in 30 minutes?"

Harlan began to wonder what rock he'd turned over.

"Sure. Thirty minutes."

It wasn't hard to spot the guy. He looked starched...serious. Like a man who never lit his own farts and would probably never see the humor in such a banal act.

Harlan flashed his shield.

"Yeah, I know who you are. We're the ones who put the fix in at city hall."

Harlan couldn't hide his surprise.

"The Bureau?"

The agent nodded stiffly.

"Let's take a walk."

He motioned Harlan to follow.

"The trail's gone cold because we want it cold. Byron Slade isn't Byron Slade."

Harlan's cop barometer hit *Storm Warning*.

"What can you tell me?"

"Well, since he apparently no longer needs our protection…"

There was a hint of graveyard humor in his voice. Maybe he could light his farts after all.

"I can open the books a little. Maybe you can pin the tail on the perp for us."

He was moving at a pretty good clip, but Harlan kept pace.

"The guy's name was Koshkanik…Boris Koshkanik. Key informant against some renegade KGB. Lot of bad blood after The Fall and they took up with the Mafia. He supplied us with names and potential threats. He was put in the Witness Protection Program three years ago."

"And that's when he popped up as Byron Slade—Agent to the Stars."

"He was a showboat. Went totally Hollywood. What can I tell you. We warned him. Stay low profile. But bloated egos like that don't last long under wraps."

They reached the edge of a parking lot.

"Got any suspects in the case?"

"This could add some names to the list."

"Keep us in the loop, O.K.?"

Harlan nodded.

"Thanks for the help."

The agent slipped on a pair of dark glasses and disappeared as quickly as he'd arrived.

45

Eddie leaned in close...a grenade nestled in the back of his eyes.
"Good sex is addicting. I know. The little head rules."
He pulled the pin.
"But you got to let her go, Harlan. She's going to take you down with her. You can't always fix things. You hang around cripples long enough and pretty soon you start to limp."
He pounded a bottle of catsup onto his scrambled eggs.
"This is L.A., man. No free lunch. Just a heap of dreams and elbows in the ribs. And, oh yeah. That ever popular course in an actor's workshop...Wrist Slitting 101."
Eddie had a case. She was high maintenance. Too much need. He had to let go...move on.... or she was going to suck him over the falls like that wave at Punta Caldera. Drown him in the killer shorebreak.
But something inside him wouldn't let go. He wanted to snap that twig that was wedged in her soul. Help her heal the abrasions she was suffering.

"I know what you're saying, Eddie. She's toxic. But this dream of hers...it gives her something to believe in at least. Something bigger than herself."

"For Christ's sake, Harlan...that's the dangerous part. Do you see the problem? This is Hollywood. These people are shells. Huge black holes of need. They never get enough attention. She's going to suck you dry. And I'm not just talking about your dick."

There was a long silence. Eddie didn't know the full story. Didn't know the Stormy Tillett that struggled inside her. Didn't taste her delicious kisses...or feel his pulse racing while they ransacked the night with the incredible passion she brought to his life.

"IA isn't going to stick this in the Cop's Closet, Harlan."

"Fuck IA. You know I've never been in sync with those control freaks."

This was going to be a tough sell. But he hated to see Harlan throw it all away.

Harlan slumped back in the booth. He cast a cold eye on the last swig of coffee as he swirled it in his cup.

"I don't mean to be a buzz-kill, man. But this little thrill ride could destroy your thirty years on the force. Zip. Nothing. All down the toilet."

Harlan gave a perfunctory nod.

"The problem is, Eddie...I'm on the down side of fifty."

Eddie felt the pain of that statement. He was no longer a kid himself.

"I'm looking at a closing window here. I know there's never going to be anyone like her again."

Eddie studied him with a new sense of urgency. This was a man who had seen the dark side of the moon...felt the breath of the Grim Reaper on his neck.

There was sympathy in his voice as he picked up the tab...threw some bills on the table.

"All I'm saying is: Watch your six, Harlan. IA is a nasty bunch. And they love their work."

"Don't worry. This isn't the hill I want to die on"

"Which hill is?"

His voice was as weary as an embattled old lion on the savanna.

"I'll know it when I see it."

46

When he arrived home she was curled on the couch in a soiled robe. Her hand tapped a precarious ash into a cold cup of coffee. She looked disgusting, pathetic.

Harlan was at the end of his rope. He'd had enough. The whole thing left a bitter taste in his mouth. His self-loathing was at a new low. For being weak. For selling out years of hard-won respect on the force. For being an accessory to her self-destruction.

"I'm not supplying you with any more of this shit."

He was pacing, agitated. He scooped up her paraphernalia, hurled it in the trash.

"One take. That's all you get in life, Lana. No one says 'Cut.' Let's do one more."

He meant it. She sensed the conviction in his voice.

"You don't understand my need," she argued. "The needle helps me forget."

But that was the problem...he *did* understand. The poison was in the wound. And the wound wouldn't heal. It was a past that would never release her. Had doomed her to self-destructive choices. And she would always be taking another hit of that crystal powder if she stayed here.

"I just can't do this any more, Lana. You gotta get clean."

She watched him coolly from across the room for several moments. Then, without a word, she rose up like a hollow-eyed zombie from the grave…walked barefoot toward him…her smooth legs swiveling like a dancer. She looked him straight in the eye. Harlan gazed back into the blue oven-heat that always kept him coming back. Then her eyes…once beginning-of-the-world blue…lit up like a refinery against the night sky.

"I can. I will," her voice whispered intensely. "Just not right now."

Her hand reached and slid the .38 from his holster. She ran her fingers across the smooth metallic finish. Then, without warning, she jammed the barrel up against his balls.

"I can pull this trigger and blast your dick right off, baby."

Her eyes were bold…defiant. There was a long tense silence. Then her tongue swirled lasciviously across her lips.

"Or I can suck it off."

She was offering him a cocktail of mind-blowing lust if he saw things her way. And if he didn't…well, the consequences could be ugly.

Her teeth bared into a nasty little smile.

"Which would you prefer?"

"God dammit!" he muttered as he felt the waves sweep on shore and wash his will out to sea. He had nothing left. The brainfire and bedlam unleashed by her burning lips…it was too much for any man to resist. Let alone a man who was running out of time.

His eyes closed and his head tilted back as she took his swollen cock into her mouth.

"I thought so," she smiled with a smug sense of victory as she finished him off once again.

* * *

But the show was over in Tinseltown. He couldn't have it both ways. If he wanted her he'd have to give up the force and get the fuck out of Dodge.

They had been the Perfect Storm…low pressure trough meeting high wind sheer. But this sexual heat between them…was it enough to survive somewhere else? Without this urban pathology…without the sick adrenaline rush of Hollywood? Could they both return to "normal"…step back from the precipice after living on the edge? Could two people with the mark of Cain return to Eden?

"We'll go somewhere…anywhere, Lana. Take that *Midnight Train to Georgia*…away from this freak show."

"I appreciate what you're doing, baby. But I didn't come here to join some Hollywood sewing circle. Everything worth doing starts out with being scared."

"Are you scared?"

"I'm terrified."

She huddled like a hummingbird up against him…her frail body shivering.

"Then let me take you home."

"I never had a home."

"Back to where I'm from."

He held her close.

"We can make it there, Lana. Make ourselves a home."

But dreams die hard. Even in the doomed. He felt something inside her still tugging at the myth. Another Dixie Stardust. Another Holly on the slab.

"That's what life is like if you want to make it in this town...waiting for the phone to ring."

"No, Lana. Life isn't something you waste sitting by a phone. It's a lot more real than that. Let's leave...together."

"Together..."

She mulled the word over as if she were hearing the last call to board a departing vessel.

"Yes. Two tickets back to Reality. We can leave tomorrow."

"But..."

He pressed his finger to her lips.

"No 'buts' this time. No more delusions. Leave everything. Meet me at the airport tomorrow night."

As he watched her waver, he decided he had to do it. He had to break the spell once and for all. One final ace to play in this high-stakes game for her fragile soul. Time was running out. He had to shatter the lingering fantasy of that sign on the hill.

"Remember what I said: *The past is never past.*"

"Yes."

"Well, there's a sheriff here from Greenville. He has a warrant."

He could see the stark terror in her eyes.

"A guy named Earl Duke?"

"Yes."

Her body shuddered as the nightmare of her past struck full force. Her voice was dry, laden with a mixture of fear and hatred.

"He was one of them," she muttered dreamlike.

The horrid sound of grackles shrieked in the back of her eyes.

She looked up at Harlan, shaken into reality by this lurid ghost from the past.

"Tomorrow night," she trembled. "I'll be there."

47

Harlan felt a jolt of panic when he got the call. It was like hearing a cough in the coffin as it entered the flames of the crematorium. His shoulder lurched.

"How?"

"He hung himself."

There was a pause on the line before the voice finished the sentence. Wondering, perhaps, if he should add what must surely sound absurd.

"With shoe laces."

Harlan had half expected it. The fissures went too deep to survive. God hadn't filled the void. And the thing that *would* fill the void…the thing he wanted most…he denied himself. Willis thought he could do that when he became a priest. Put an end to all the cravings of the flesh. But this was *the swamp* he was messing with…a billion-year-old energy force working him day and night. Whispering to him in every passing skirt. He was in the path of an eighteen wheeler and no quaint incantations in front of an altar were going to change that. He was just road kill waiting to happen.

Harlan tried to picture the scene of his boyhood friend dangling from a beam…the shoelaces constricting the last desperate breath from his constricted body. The shock of disbelief still frozen in his eyes…realizing too late that his entire life had been wasted. All his choices had been wrong. And there was no going back.

Harlan hung up the phone as the image lingered in his mind.

In a way it was a relief after witnessing the tortured creature at the asylum. The man he had seen there was clearly a shell. After his take down in the corridor he was reduced to being a lab rat. And it was written on his face. There was nothing but death left inside him.

The agony was over. He had…with a pair of shoelaces…detached himself from the pain of all his unrealized desire. He floated free now of the grief his wanting had caused him…of being locked inside this flawed human shell.

* * *

There seemed to be a sacrificial element in the human mind that went against all survival instincts. Something bent on self-destruction as a form of punishment for all one's failings. Penance for all the accumulated insults a man must suffer every day. For most it became day-to-day hair shirt punishment of neglect and indifference.

But sometimes it came as a sudden impulse…desperately charging into enemy fire with a sense of one's own immortality. For Willis…watching his hunger snarling back at him every day in the mirror…it became a violent need to end the anguish. Either way…they all end up DOA.

Harlan picked up an apple. He took a bite of its crisp red flesh…savored the sweetness of the juices flowing across his tongue.

The human mind is an odd duck. Separate it from the wisdom of the body and you're in for a shitload of trouble. He should have known that. He should have known a pair of lace panties always trumps half-assed attempts at celibacy.

48

Harlan paced in the harsh light of the terminal. He glanced at his watch. Eleven forty-five. The second hand moved in short bursts across the numbers...precious seconds disappearing and still no sign of Lana.

She should have been here thirty minutes ago. It had to be tonight. Tomorrow would be too late. For both of them. He unfolded the Wanted poster...gazed at it darkly.

The net was closing. He was finished as a cop and he knew it. Internal Affairs was closing in. He'd already left his shield behind. And that blood hound lawman from Carolina was closing fast. By morning it would be over.

This was their only out. Scrap the job. Blow this joint. Start over with a clean slate. He should have done it sooner.

A surge of hope quickened his pulse at the thought of a fresh start. Like a *Spring Peeper* when he was a kid. Tiny thumbnail-sized frogs that rocked the woods with celebration at the first sign of spring. They lay dormant all winter, surviving the cold with their own natural antifreeze. And when spring approached they woke up the whole neighborhood. Life was resurgent again.

But the mood evaporated as he watched the clock. Could they really make it trying to return to the past? Or was it just a charade the mind played when it yearns for the long lost safety of home.

For her it wouldn't be home exactly. But it had the feel of some place safe he'd known long ago. She needed that. A sanctuary where she could heal.

* * *

His cell phone rang.

"Eddie?"

There was a long pause on the other end. The voice was strangely distant, cloistered in some emotional vacuum.

"You'd better come over here, Harlan."

"It's over for me, Eddie. I'm waiting for Lana now. We're leaving this town. Starting over."

"It's about Lana, Harlan."

Now there was a darker edge to Eddie's voice.

It sent a chill through Harlan's gut.

"What about her?"

"You'd better come over."

"Where are you?"

"Larrabee."

"I'm on my way."

There was another pause.

"It gets worse."

"What do you mean?"

"There's a dead sheriff at her place."

Harlan crumpled the Wanted poster…tossed it to the ground as he raced through the terminal. It suddenly seemed cold and empty...a surreal dreamscape...everything moving in slow motion.

He hit the gas out of the airport. His head was throbbing, his mind spinning as he rolled onto the 405. He slid through traffic and into the fast lane, foot hard on the pedal. Snaking past cars on Sunset, he felt some leaden force...like gravity sucking him over the edge...deep into the void of a black hole. Then he turned up Larrabee.

Flashing red lights skewered the night.

Eddie saw him coming, blocked his path. Behind him, the paramedics rolled a gurney out of the apartment. Her arm dangled limply from under a sheet, an oxygen mask covered her face.

"She's in a coma, Harlan. They're doing all they can."

Harlan stood dazed, disbelieving. Like some sleepwalker he pushed past Eddie and approached the gurney. Gently, he lifted Lana's pale arm and slipped it back under the sheet.

As he did he took one long last look at her...the beautiful face that had first peered at him from beneath a black umbrella. The acetylene blue fire that burned so bright was now gone from those eyes. The liquid pools of blue had turned dull and distant.

"She's special," his voice quavered. "Take good care of her."

The medics nodded, pushed the gurney into the ambulance and sped off into the night.

* * *

Harlan felt like a child who realizes too late he is swimming in the deep end of the pool. His emotions sucked him down into the cool embrace of denial. This wasn't happening. It was a dream.

But it was only the beginning. That night he would take a ride in the Black Car like he could never have imagined. Down the slippery coastal road along the cliff's edge. And then it would hit him as he plunged over the edge and into the sea.

He felt himself succumb to some deep well of grief. Like that wave that held him under at Punta Caldera that day. He could feel himself drowning...fighting for every breath. Struggling against the grip of death.

There is something terribly wrong here, he told himself. He was a cop. He saw death every day. He was numb to it. But this was new. What had Lana stirred in him? He had never felt such deep emotions before. And he could not control it. His gut began wrenching. Spasms that rose from deep in the recesses of ancient memory.

Even when his father died the loss was conceded...but not this deeply grieved. Family had never been a strong centerpiece for Harlan. But now...the way this grief space split open his gut...grabbed him and shook him with menace...he felt a link severed...a link he never knew he had.

*There is no more...there is no more...*played inside his head as if for the very first time. Struck him dumb as he watched the gurney trundle past and the overwhelming gravity of what it meant.

Death was an end so final...a silence so profound...that there was no way to deal with it rationally. It went beyond the cool click of ivory on velvet green. No more laughter. No more touch. No more tenderness. Just void. Stilled, undiminished nothingness.

The spark of life had been extinguished. The very private bond they had shared...severed. The earth had lost one of its kind to air and dust. Anything that final...the absolute obliteration of a life...must be dealt with by forces lodged far deeper than he had ever known before.

* * *

"Eddie," he muttered.

Eddie appeared at his side.

"Yeah."

"Look after her, would you? Till I get there."

He fought the burning in his shoulder...the burning that surged upward now into his eyes.

"I need to check inside."

Eddie nodded in understanding.

"You got it, pal."

* * *

Harlan entered the apartment where he and Lana had once set the earth on fire. As he stood there he felt the air sucked out of the room. It wasn't the same now. It was no longer the lush rainforest where they had gorged their senses with pleasure. Now he was gazing across fields of ash. *The suffocation of the spirit can do terrible things to people.*

There was dark shape on the floor. A pool of blood surrounded it. It was the Carolina sheriff. He had a butcher knife in his back.

The Crime Scene Unit was gathering evidence.

"What have you got?" Harlan asked.

"We're still putting the pieces together. Looks like he tried to assault her. She caught him in the gut several times...then planted it in his back to make sure."

He shook his head at the violence of the knife wounds.

"Lot of pent-up rage."

Harlan nodded. He understood better than anyone where that rage came from.

* * *

He wandered the room, trying to replay the events. He touched the things that seemed so familiar...her white bible...her *Casablanca* poster...her magazine clipping of Lana Turner she had unfolded so reverently at the Pantages.

The rhododendron sat wilted in the window...brackish and dying.

Like a camera filming the scene he began to piece it together. On the bed a suitcase she had been packing. Some clothes...shoes...a make-up kit. She was almost ready for takeoff.

Then the phone rang. She goes to answer it. An agent. No dice. The role she wanted has gone to someone else. Maybe next time. But Lana had run out of "next times." She gazed bitterly at the stack of headshots sitting by the phone. That sweet Hollywood smile suddenly began to mock her. She grabs one...tears it to shreds.

Then a knock on the door. The Sheriff from Carolina. Come to take her away. He forces his way in. She resists. He seizes her. There's a struggle. Somehow she manages to grab a kitchen knife. Plunges it into his gut. Again. And again. His eyes go stark...in shock. He reels back. Clutches his gut as blood pours out. His intestines exposed. He tumbles back onto the floor. Still filled with rage...with flashes of her childhood...this very man...Earl Duke grunting on top of her...she plunges the knife deep into his back. And that's where he dies...in a pool of his own blood.

And then she clutched her white Bible to her chest for solace.

Harlan picked it up. A marker held the place she had last opened it. Some inspirational verse that would bring her a sense of peace? He flipped it open and his heart sank.

It was peace all right. In the hollowed out center was a freshly used syringe. Spoon. Rubber tubing. And the last remnants of white powder. Street junk. Enough for a lethal dose.

He felt sick as he stared at the words *Holy Bible* embossed in gold on the cover.

Her voice kept playing over and over in his head.
"This bible will keep me safe," she had assured herself.
"God damn it!" he muttered.

* * *

Perhaps it was an illusion that he could ever really come to know her. Let alone save her. He fell prey to her instincts...to that heat...the splendor of those eyes. Blue lightning...raw and full of larceny...throwing his critical faculties into disorder...where appetite outranked restraint.

Lana was different. She had something special. Some uncut gem inside her. The others were copies. But she was the thing itself. She could never be one of them. The glitterati of Sunset and Vine. He knew it. And deep down he felt she knew it. He tried to tell her it didn't matter. But to her it was all that mattered.

And all the stars
that never were
are parking cars
and pumping gas...

Or turning tricks on La Brea.

Very few knew the way back to San Jose. Mostly they just spun like coins...neither heads nor tails...up and down the soiled Walk of Fame. Until they rolled into the gutter and disappeared. Still unknown. Still waiting by the phone. And still parking cars.

* * *

The Black Car roared to life...sped through the night...winding upward into the Hollywood Hills. Headlights sliced bleak contorted shapes out of the darkness as he rounded each curve.

At the top Harlan braked the car near the edge of a steep incline. He left the engine idling...looked out over the glittering town that had just claimed another victim. The sign stood below him...large letters silhouetted against the glowing metropolis below. The "H" loomed like some giant theme park come-on...the entrance to a two-bit freak show...inviting you in for cheap thrills.

For Harlan this sign had become the enemy...an emblem of evil. It stood there mocking him...a grim reminder of the power it wielded...the lives it had so callously destroyed. "H" is for Heartless. "H" is for Hollow. "H" is for the bottomless despair endured in this honeyed Hell.

From his car radio rose a beautiful operatic voice...*Chi il bel sogno di Doretta*. It plunged into him like a hypodermic...filled him like a junkie shooting up on crystal pain.

He stepped out of the car...strode down the hill until the "H" loomed large in front of him. There it was...lit up in the bright glare of floodlights for all the dreamers below...glittering with the well-scrubbed promise of fame. But up close he could see what the others were blind to...all the blemishes...cheap tattered clapboard...peeling paint. It was the same Hollywood he saw up close every day. All the ugliness...the sleaze...the callous disregard of a town that destroyed fragile lives like Lana's.

Harlan shook with rage. It was something he'd wanted to do for a long, long time. Something he should have done years ago. He yanked out his .38. His hand quaked violently as he pulled the trigger and pumped six rounds into the heartless beast. Blam! Blam! Blam! He cursed and screamed at the top of his lungs as the rounds spun from the barrel and ripped into the sign. Blam! Blam! Blam!

Then he sank to his knees…helpless…as the last echo of the shots were soaked up by the emptiness of the night…the dry arid soul of L.A.

49

The doctor came in…checked her vitals. It would be touch and go he said. She might make it. All they could do was wait.

He watched the peaceful expression on Lana's face as the respirator hissed in the background. It was almost angelic…that gentle curve of her lips. As if she was still waiting for the phone to ring. As if it still might happen.

Deep down he knew it was a trapeze act. They both knew. That's one thing he liked about her. That voice in the back of the head saying: "I can't go on…I'll go on."

And she knew what held it all together was this hunger they both felt…this hunger every time their bodies embraced. She had lead him into a forest. Dark and deep and scented with the fragrance of ancient rain-soaked dreams.

"See you at the movies, baby…see you at the movies."

* * *

Hollywood was a place where you think you know the rules, but you don't.

Much more frequent in Hollywood than the emergence of Cinderella, is her sudden vanishing.

Ben Hecht saw them languishing in the shadows even way back then.

Harlan McCoy never understood this disease…this pathetic effort to immortalize oneself. This fixation with anything so barren, empty, and meaningless as fame. It was *The Thing That Would Not Happen* that would kill her. It was always there in her…great collisions of opportunity missed by mere seconds. In the subtext of every unreturned call.

The same void that had killed Holly. Peg Entwhistle. And all the others. The failed dream. Unable to let go. To just be.

He watched her there in a coma. An angel fallen from the sky. A slim young girl with dark flowing hair. And sacred gemstone eyes the color of heaven.

He wanted to tell her about tiny victories. Small victories each day that make one's life unique. The tiny successes that please us…sunshine on skin…the smell of the sea…the touch of someone close…

This is how we must measure our lives he would say. This is what makes it real. Not the glittering lights. Not fleeting fame. But these tiny, intimate, personal victories. This is what really matters.

He wasn't sure he would get the chance.

As he left the hospital something thick was in the air. A tremor in the sky that signaled *chubasco*.

50

Harlan pressed down on the accelerator. He was feeling good. He aimed his car into the void of the desert and drove. The highway opened up before him...a black asphalt ribbon that stretched out as if it had no end.

Sixty...seventy...eighty...the slim arm of the speedometer arched into the red...the pistons pounded out more and more power...squeezing every ounce of explosive fuel into vapor...until the high-pitched whine seemed to satisfy something inside him.

But his foot pressed harder still. Ninety...one-hundred...one-hundred-ten. The desert became a blur. The tires seared across the surface of the hot asphalt. Harlan was inside a bullet. And God help anything that crossed his path...

He was not stopping. Not now. Not when he needed to feel the wondrous freedom of full flight...

* * *

A downpour had just cleansed the sky. The sun beamed rich and molten…dusting sagebrush with a mantle of gold. A dazzling display of crimson tinted the clouds like a grassfire as it began to set.

"Perfect Hollywood ending, don't you think?"

He looked over at her.

"Did I tell you I got a call from Eddie?"

"Forensics said it was a Russian hit after all. Slade's past caught up with him."

The hot wind swirled at Harlan's temples. He took a deep breath of desert air.

"Lucky for us they eat their own, huh?"

A small chuckle. He was feeling relaxed now that he had left it all behind.

"Imagine that. Actually suspecting you might have done it."

His banter was relaxed and easy as they sped across the flatlands.

"You're going to like it where I live. It's down to earth…authentic. A good land…with good people in it. Just open sky and the sweetest water you'll ever taste. People wave 'Hello.' And you never have to lock your door. And it doesn't matter if you ever become famous…because people are happy with who they are."

Harlan was on a roll. The warm wind reminded him of home. And he felt a need to tell her about it.

"We can go up this hill where I used to stand on warm nights. And you can feel the softness of the desert breeze on your face. And gaze up at a million stars."

He paused a moment in recollection of those times.

"There's a deep sense of peace out there."

***

A tumbleweed ambled lazily across the road in front of him. As it passed Harlan thought he saw something in the distance. A dark shape. Like the blue-black sheen of a raven's wing. He blinked in the slanting rays of the sun. But it was nothing.

He pressed the accelerator harder.

He looked over at where she sat. He saw her again on their trip up the coast to Santa Barbara that day. The wind blowing her hair through the open window. Her eyes closed…a serene smile on her face. Her long skirt ruffling in the breeze…revealing smooth tan thighs.

He smiled with satisfaction.

"And the lightning storms. Yes, baby, you'll love the beautiful lightning storms…"

Harlan had been altered irrevocably by Lana. Lost in the dark raptures of her appetite, he had gained a greater sympathy for people like Willis. A different man had been created. One with a deeper appreciation for the brevity of being.

There was so much he wanted to leave behind. All the black ruins of his life. The sulfur skies. The swarming traffic. The silent screams of blue-armed junkies shooting up in the night…struggling to escape their anonymity. But especially all the lies enshrined in that sign on the hill. Lies that lured the Lanas of the world to the altar of this false God.

And the Black Car. Yes. That horrid *thump*. Most of all he wanted to leave that behind.

They were making good time now. Putting a lot of distance between them and L.A.

"I'm glad you recovered…it looked bad for awhile…but you showed 'em what you're made of."

Harlan smiled with satisfaction and drove silently for a long time.

***

Dusk was settling in and a golden glow lay across the land. It began defining textures across the surface...new shapes that swirled and swept past him.

Then suddenly...there it was again. That black shape. It seemed to be bearing down on them.

It sent a chill through Harlan.

***

Until this moment...driving across open desert with Lana...he felt he might have left that Black Car behind. Made a clean getaway from the past. But now he feared there would always be a Black Car out there...roaring out of the dark of night. Black on black...bearing down on him. Like the blind, dull bullet that had taken him down that day.

It was the violence of the times and Harlan had tried to put it all in the Cop's Closet. But the closet was full. Spilling over with the horrors of thirty years on the force...chalk marks around the mangled lives, the corrosive despair, the echo of slaughter-house screams in a savage species.

He began to understand the source of his dream. Why that huge black Packard kept plunging down a rain-slick highway. He saw who the driver was now. What the shadows were that crossed the road. The terrible truth behind that *thump*. Who the body was that slammed across the windshield.

It was the reckless journey in each of us. The dark side of being human. It was all the brute force let loose upon the world. Ruination stalking us at every instant of our life. Waiting for us always. Swerving the corner as we stepped off the curb. Silver grillwork grinning with menace. It's dark shape speeding into the distance…and the softness left dying in its path.

* * *

He glanced over at Lana beside him…seeking reassurance from her youth and beauty. But his expression turned stricken.

All that lay on the seat was an 8 x 10 head shot.

His shoulder lurched as he gripped the wheel and roared into the gathering night. Only the last slanting rays spread over the open desert now. From the photo her warm eyes seemed to watch him. And he could still see the yearning…the search for the source of her sorrow that it might finally be put to rest. The hurt of one who never quite understood the wanton destruction of innocence.

Cherish the remnants of softness, they were saying. *The rest is nothing.*

And then the wind curled in through the window…caught the photo and swept it out onto the desert currents of air.

A small dust-devil hurled it across open desert. It bounced and danced along the sand with a new found sense of freedom.

Harlan watched it in the rearview mirror billowing in the company of tumbleweeds. He watched it disappear in the distance…still bearing the message she had written across it for all her future fans…

See you at the movies!
Love, Lana

Printed in the United States
57259LVS00002B/19-27